Y0-AGK-324

Looking Into You

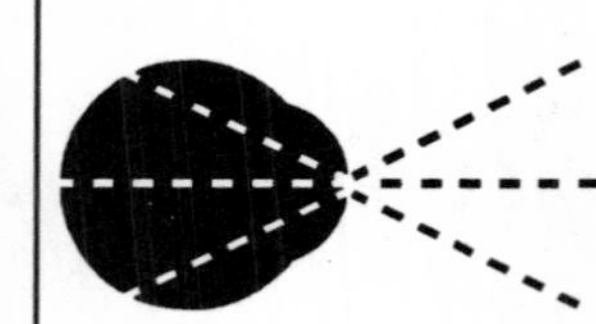

This Large Print Book carries the Seal of Approval of N.A.V.H.

Looking Into You

Chris Fabry

THORNDIKE PRESS
A part of Gale, Cengage Learning

Farmington Hills, Mich • San Francisco • New York • Waterville, Maine
Meriden, Conn • Mason, Ohio • Chicago

Thorndike Press, a part of Gale, Cengage Learning.

Thorndike Press® Large Print Christian Fiction.
The text of this Large Print edition is unabridged.
Other aspects of the book may vary from the original edition.
Set in 16 pt. Plantin.

LIBRARY OF CONGRESS CATALOGING-IN-PUBLICATION DATA

Names: Fabry, Chris, 1961– author.
Title: Looking into you / by Chris Fabry.
Description: Large print edition. | Waterville, Maine : Thorndike Press, 2017. | Series: Thorndike Press large print Christian fiction
Identifiers: LCCN 2017012261| ISBN 9781432839604 (hardcover) | ISBN 1432839608 (hardcover)
Subjects: LCSH: Mothers and daughters—Fiction. | Adoption—Fiction. | Single women—Fiction. | Large type books. | GSAFD: Christian fiction.
Classification: LCC PS3556.A26 L66 2017 | DDC 813/.54—dc23
LC record available at https://lccn.loc.gov/2017012261

Published in 2017 by arrangement with Tyndale House Publishers, Inc.

Printed in the United States of America
1 2 3 4 5 6 7 21 20 19 18 17

To Rose and Chris Couch, with love

Prologue

There is no greater power on earth than a mother's love.

I'd been staring at the words on the screen, at the blinking cursor following them like a tapping foot, for what felt like hours when I heard familiar voices outside my office in the English department of Millhaven College.

"Think about it. Her mother is out there somewhere." Ginny Baylor, an economics professor.

"It's haunting," the second voice agreed. Madalyn Palmer, from admissions.

I opened my door.

"I thought you were on sabbatical," Madalyn said when she saw me. "Off in the mountains or to a beach house near your parents."

"Just getting a change of scenery," I said. "Get the juices flowing."

"How's the writing going?" Ginny said, a

little too much concern on her face. "Any progress?"

"I suppose it depends on how you define *progress.*"

They smiled at me, though it felt more sad than reassuring. Like they could tell I was no further along with my dissertation than when I'd begun my sabbatical.

"What were you talking about?" I said.

The elevator opened and Ginny excused herself. Something about a dinner appointment. Madalyn inched closer.

"We saw a documentary last night that is the most heartbreaking thing. And you know how picky I am about films."

I nodded. "What film?"

She told me the title, the art theater where it was playing, and I catalogued the information. Then in rapid fire, she summarized a film that began as the story of residents in a nursing home but gradually shifted focus to a remarkable girl who worked with them. A girl adopted at birth and then abandoned, who passed through the system of child protective services like water through a drain. A girl with an extraordinary gift for connecting to those whose minds were seemingly beyond reach. A girl who had been deeply damaged by choices made before her birth. My heart beat faster and catching breath was a struggle.

"Paige, you have to see it," Madalyn said. "It's all I've been able to think about."

"It sounds good," I said, choking a little.

Madalyn shook her head again as if she couldn't get the lingering images from her mind. As she stepped into the elevator, I asked the question that had floated to the surface of my heart.

"Do they mention her name?" I said. "The girl in the film?"

"Yes. You never see her face. They blur it for anonymity, I guess. They just show her eyes. They have this movement — they call it something; I can't remember. But her name is Treha. Isn't that exotic?"

"Yes," I managed.

I limped back to the office and closed the door and leaned hard against it, sliding to the floor. No overwhelming emotion gripped me. I simply struggled to breathe. My eyes fell on a set of books. My greatest treasures. The stories that made my heart come alive.

I crawled on all fours to the desk and pulled myself up into the wooden chair. Ten minutes earlier I had thought my biggest problem was my dissertation. The working title was "The Strength of a Mother's Love: A Literary Epistemology." The last words

I'd written still hung on the screen: *There is no greater power on earth than a mother's love.*

"Unless it's a mother's fear," I whispered.

I found the trailer online and watched it. I read reviews. I searched for another explanation, a plausible denial, some excuse. And finally I bought a ticket and slipped into the back row of the theater to watch a film about my daughter.

CHAPTER 1

Miriam

Exiting the dorm elevator, her arms loaded down with plastic bags, Miriam Howard froze at the sound of the raised voice coming from the RA's room.

"I don't mind rooming with a freshman. I don't mind not getting my requested roommate. But I draw the line at rooming with a freak!"

"Shelly, she's not a freak. Don't talk that way. She's not even a freshman."

The door closed but Miriam could still hear them.

"She has the personality of an end table, Jill. She won't look at me when I speak to her. It's like talking to a houseplant."

"You've wanted a room to yourself," Jill said. "Think of it that way. You won't have to make small talk."

Miriam closed her eyes. She liked the RA, Jill, but she could tell whoever made room assignments hadn't fully comprehended Treha's situation. Back in the spring Miriam had flown to Tennessee with Treha and met with the dean of admissions to describe the special circumstances. She'd gone on a tour of the Bethesda campus and the dormitory. Treha, she was told, would be nurtured and helped to become all she could be. And under no circumstances would the faculty or administration exploit Treha's semicelebrity status. In fact, only a few on campus had even seen the documentary that featured her story. Treha's secret was safe.

Would Treha be safe, though? That was the question that drew Miriam to the girl when she had first met her. She had hired Treha at Desert Gardens because the girl seemed so vulnerable and yet so competent with the older residents. As Treha's story had unfolded, Miriam had grown more attached to her and had taken on a motherly role that had brought her all the way to Tennessee to help Treha in her next steps.

Earlier today, when they'd flown in from Tucson, Miriam had returned from the Enterprise rental counter to find Treha standing at the start of the baggage claim carousel, alone and inconspicuous. She'd studied the girl, trying to see her through a stranger's eyes. Treha had certainly made progress with . . . What would she call it? Her condition? Her disability? The medication prescribed along with the exercise and diet had helped the girl lose weight. Her nystagmus, an involuntary eye movement, had improved, and those who didn't look closely wouldn't notice.

Still, there was no question that Treha was different. Miriam hated the word. It was a category, a way of pigeonholing. *Different* meant "challenged" or "special." None of the words came close to describing Treha and what she faced in life or in attending college alone.

She walked to the RA's door and stood there, listening, about to knock when something rose up inside. Something that told her to turn and leave, to let them work it out. This was no longer her job. A bird must flap its wings in the wind alone.

Miriam took the bags to Treha's room. "All right, I got some tissues and a few pieces of silverware in case you want a snack in your room and —" she shook out the pillowcase — "you'll want to wash this before you sleep on it. You remember where the laundry is, right?"

Treha nodded. She was on the corner of her bed wearing her scrubs, preferring them to jeans — another of the girl's quirks. "I don't think my roommate likes me."

Miriam kept unloading the bags. "Well, she doesn't know you yet."

Treha held a folded piece of paper, turning it over and over.

"What do you have there?" Miriam said, sitting beside her.

"I found it as I was unpacking."

She handed her the note and Miriam recognized her husband's scrawl. She tried to act casual about it as if she'd read the words before, but she really handed it back because her eyes were too blurry. Just the thought of Charlie taking this step moved her. But right now everything moved her. The girl had awakened something in him, too.

"They don't make them like Charlie anymore, do they?" Treha said.

Miriam laughed. "No, they sure don't. Charlie opened up a little sliver of his heart for you. I think you're in there forever."

Treha folded the note and put it back in her suitcase and zipped the flap. The suitcase was gigantic — a gift from one of the Desert Gardens residents, Elsie Pratt. The old woman had taken Treha under her wing and been the one to recommend that Treha attend Bethesda, her alma mater. With the savings Elsie had left, she could afford to send Treha to the school for at least a year. Miriam and Charlie had matched her commitment, and with the year Treha had from the community college . . . Well, they would cross the senior year bridge when they came to it. The lawsuit against the company responsible for Treha's condition had paid for her treatment, but in a cruel twist, Treha had received nothing else.

There was so much unfairness in the girl's life. So much loss. She had no idea who or where her mother was. She had been tossed about on the sea of the foster care system and hadn't been able to walk on water. Now Miriam was losing control over who would interact with her, who might say something cutting or mean.

Deep breath. Lines rehearsed. Miriam wiped her eyes and set her jaw.

"All right, you have my number. Anything you need, anytime you have a question, or if you just want to talk, you know how to reach me. And you have Charlie's e-mail."

Treha fidgeted with the hem of her scrubs top. In one motion she turned and hugged Miriam, burying her head in the woman's chest, and Miriam thought her heart would burst.

She leaned back and took Treha's face in her hands. "Treha, I'm going to be honest. I don't want you to go to this school or any other. I want you to stay with us at Desert Gardens. I want you to live with Charlie and me. I'd like to keep you for myself, let you keep going to the community college. But somehow that doesn't seem fair. To you or the rest of the world."

Treha nodded.

"It's not going to be easy to fit in here and find your place. Finding a friend might be hard. But just because it's hard doesn't mean it can't be done. You know that."

Miriam picked up her purse and checked the room once more. Her work was done. Or maybe it was just beginning. This was every parent's nightmare and worst fear, turning to leave and not looking back. She wasn't Treha's mother. She hadn't raised her. Treha hadn't been in her life long enough for it to hurt this much.

She turned back to Treha. "When your head hits the pillow every night, know that there are two old dogs in Arizona praying for you, a couple of hours behind you. And when you wake up every morning, you pray for us. We're going to need it. Okay?"

Miriam kissed Treha on the forehead and walked out of the room, willing herself not to turn again.

Chapter 2

Paige

"Paige, we have a problem," Dr. Waldron said with a wheezy rasp.

A comb-over made the head of Millhaven's English department appear somewhat Dickensian, without the spectacles or coal on the fire. I had to resist focusing on the hair growing from his ears that made me want to Secret Santa him a pair of tweezers.

"Do *we* have a problem or do *I* have a problem?" I said.

"*We* have a problem because *I* am committed to your success."

I tapped my pen against my leg, the pen my father had made me during my family's years as missionaries. Late in the evening when his translation work was put aside and he'd finished helping village men fix leaking roofs or butcher wild pigs, he would steal away to his workbench made from two fallen trees and chip at wood, fashioning trinkets to send to supporters. I would sit with him by the dim light and watch him work until my eyes grew heavy, my chin on the edge of the tree trunk.

"Words are the secret things of God," he said one night as he carried me to bed. Deep in the night, if I listen closely enough, I can still hear his voice, whispers of prayers and stories lost in the jungle.

My pen long ago ran out of ink and I have not been able to find the refill cartridge that will fit. Still, I hold it as part talisman, part connection with my past.

Dr. Waldron glanced at the tapping pen, then gestured to a stack of pages on the edge of the desk. There were several stacks. His office looked like the eternal resting place for trees. "That stack is from professors with PhDs who want to teach here. Qualified and motivated instructors who have rigorously pursued their academic careers and who see this school as a good fit."

"And I don't fit any longer."

"I didn't say that. You fit well."

"But my inability to finish my doctorate has hampered my long-term employment prospects."

He folded aged hands. "It's not just one thing, Paige. And it's not your inability to finish your thesis. It's your inability to *begin.* You spent all of last year on a sabbatical that yielded very little, from what you're saying."

"Writing is not simply page count, Dr. Waldron."

"No, it's research and thought along with sitting in the chair." He punched a finger at an air keyboard. "But you're hedging again."

I tried not to flinch. "I'm stuck. You're right. I've followed the trail of my original idea to a dead end."

"Then just start. Move toward a thought that interests you. Do *something.* It's been seven years. Other schools would probably allow you to string things along a few more, but I don't think that's fair to you or those in this stack. Or your students, for that matter."

"What else is hampering me? You said this isn't the only thing."

He waved a hand. "You seem divided."

I closed my eyes to keep from rolling them in front of him. "Is this about the class I'm teaching at Bethesda? It's one night a week. It's material I already teach here. And contact with those students will invigorate me."

"You need to be invigorated by your thesis."

"So you're telling me I should cancel?"

"No."

"Are you giving me a deadline?"

"Maybe that's what you need, Paige. Maybe instead of a longer leash and an open-ended process, you need someone to put their foot down. Or just give you a swift kick in the behind."

"Publish or perish," I said, completing his thought.

"No. Not publish or perish. Move. Rise from the stagnant water. You have a gift. I've seen it. But we're enabling you by allowing this to continue."

Hoping my face still showed composure, I nodded. "What's the deadline?"

"End of semester. Get me the first draft by then. What's the title again?"

I hesitated, then blurted out the title, cringing a little at the "mother's love" part.

"Good. Don't think about it any longer. Put it down. Put your notes away. Write."

The walls felt like they were moving inward as we spoke. I debated my next question, not sure if I wanted the answer. "And what happens if I don't? What happens if I remain stuck?"

He stood and walked in front of the desk to lean against it, arms folded. He was wearing house shoes, I kid you not. Dearfoams slippers with a hole in the toe. I had the same ones, though not as worn.

"*Stuck* is a choice. *Stuck* is saying you're afraid to be wrong. *Stuck* is no longer an option. If you have to cancel the Bethesda class to use that time, do it."

"I can't back out of that commitment."

"Then show me you take this seriously. Do the work."

He punctuated the last three words with an outstretched index finger. And then he said it again, wagging the finger in my face. "Write it."

"What do you think is holding you back, Paige?"

Ron Gleason delivered the question as if the words could harmonize with the clanging silverware and barely audible string music that was the subtext of our meal.

"I mean with your dissertation," he said when I didn't respond.

Men hate conversational dead space. Women thrive on the rests. They wait. They listen. They lean in. For women, questions are launching pads to the heart. For men, they're shots toward a target you hit and move on to the next, like a conversational biathlon.

I took a sip of decaf that I wished were

wine. I needed something with bite.

"You've been working on it for years," he continued as if I didn't know this. "Did you get anything done during the sabbatical?"

"Not much," I admitted.

He smiled, a mix of sympathy and confusion. Invitation to explain further, which I didn't want to do. I don't know what had made me tell him about the meeting with Dr. Waldron. I suppose I needed to share it with someone, but I was questioning that decision now.

I studied Ron's hands, folded on the table. An academic's hands, small-boned and smooth. They fit his stature — he was diminutive, to put it kindly, but well-built and muscular. He worked out, ran the trail near Bethesda, where he taught math and physics, and even competed in long-distance runs. A few years younger than me — he'd been a freshman when I graduated from Bethesda, so I hadn't known him — he was mature and godly. That had quickly become clear when he'd joined the small-group Bible study I attended. Someone arranged for us to sit near each other on that first night, then invited us to parties or Thanksgiving or Christmas celebrations as if we were a project, as if mere proximity might lead to a relationship.

The matchmaking efforts annoyed me, but I couldn't deny I liked Ron's company, much as I might've wanted to. What he lacked in size, he made up for in heart. But it wasn't *his* heart I questioned.

I picked at my blackened chicken and asparagus and didn't look Ron in the eye. The choice of this restaurant was much too expensive for my level of commitment.

"I'd like to ask you something," he said, again breaking the silence. I put down my fork and wiped at phantom crumbs, dreading the words I assumed he would say.

"We've known each other for quite a while, Paige. Since the moment we met, I've known there was something special about you. And as I've gotten to know you better, that feeling has increased. You're amazing. A brilliant mind. A beautiful smile. There's nothing about you that doesn't fascinate me. You've probably heard that before."

"Oh, a million times," I said with a wave of a hand, and he laughed.

"I wanted to bring you here tonight and ask the next logical question. About us moving forward. Your sabbatical is over. The new semester's begun. It's a perfect time to make a decision."

In his mathematical mind, everything was a theorem or postulate. A + B = C. C − B

= A. And so forth.

"Decision?" I said.

"About the future. For us. I believe there is one. Can you see us being more than friends?"

(2A) × (B − ME) = Marriage.

I placed my napkin in my lap and took a sip of water and tried to focus. "Ron, don't you think we're too old for this?"

"Old for what?"

"Maybe you're not, but I feel like I am."

"Too old for love?"

"For dating or getting our hearts broken. For change. I'm cement that was poured decades ago. I'm set. I have a life I've carved out in teaching and with my home."

"That sounds like giving up. You're barely forty, Paige."

"It's realism. I've embraced my singleness, like you. Isn't that what you've encouraged people to do? I've heard of your talks to the students in chapel."

"I've always prayed, 'Not my will but yours,' when it comes to being single. But, Paige, as I've prayed, I feel like the Lord has brought you back time and again."

"And how am I supposed to argue with God?"

"I'm not asking you to argue with him. I'm asking you to open your heart to the possibility that he wants to work on both of us. I think we could be good for each other."

I sighed. "Ron, you think you know me, but you don't."

He nodded. "Which is why I'm asking to go to the next level. I want to know you better."

"Even if we were perfectly matched, a relationship takes a lot of work."

He pushed his plate away and went full bore, gesturing with his hands. "You're right. It will be a lot of work. And it's scary for me. You're not the only concrete that's set. But over the past few months I haven't been able to get away from the possibility that there might be something good for us. I think it's worth taking another step." His passion was sort of cute, the way he sat up in his chair like he had graduated from the children's table in the kitchen to the adult table in the dining room.

I smiled and a warmth I didn't desire filled me, making me fumble the next words. "I . . . I'm fond of you, Ron. I really am. For most women, you're a dream. They would kill to have someone like you interested in them."

"But not you."

"Don't give me that look."

He straightened. "Don't try to control my

feelings."

"See? We're fighting already and we haven't even started a deeper relationship."

He stifled a smile.

"Full disclosure," I said. "There are things about my life that would cause you to doubt how amazing I am."

"That's full disclosure?"

"It's a start. And it's true."

He reached a hand across the table and took one of mine. "I want to get to know you. But you have to let me in."

My cheeks flushed, but I pulled my hand back and looked at my lap, my napkin, the design on the tablecloth, the carpet. There was a piece of bread on the floor, presumably from the last diners who sat at this table. Funny what you miss when you're not in crisis.

"Can we talk about something else?" I said.

"Paige," Ron said softly. "What could be so bad? Were you abused? Did you plagiarize an essay? Have a relationship with a student? Knock off a convenience store? What do you think I can't handle?"

I looked into his warm brown eyes and imagined the words spilling out. *I have a child I've never met. I gave her up and never made contact, even once I knew she wanted to know me. I could've easily found her months ago, but I haven't moved toward her and probably never will. Do you want this kind of heart beside you the rest of your life?*

Instead of saying this and a thousand other things to push him away, I went the safe route.

"Let me pray about it," I said.

"Fair enough." He said it sadly and we ate in silence, except for the tinkling of fine silverware that sounded like regret.

CHAPTER 3

Treha

Treha sat alone in a corner of the dining hall, listening to the conversations around her and feeling the clothes she was wearing scratch at her back and neck. She would rather wear scrubs, but those weren't on the approved apparel list.

So far she'd resisted the urge to call Miriam about her roommate or the way she felt during orientation or the fact that not one person had spoken directly to her except for those who were paid to do so. Even those people seemed mystified by her. Almost afraid, as if they would catch something if they got too close. She held out hope that once classes started tomorrow, things would be different. She would get into a rhythm of reading and studying that would ground her. Maybe her adviser would help. Maybe she would find a friend. Maybe the world would end and she wouldn't have to worry about any of this.

A girl wearing black glasses with lenses in the shape of cats' eyes walked through the dining hall, stopping at a table to say something. The whole table broke into laughter and the girl moved forward without a smile. Barely five feet tall, she looked top-heavy, as if her large bosom would topple her. But her wide hips prevented this. Her dark hair was pulled back and held in place by a colorful headband. To Treha's surprise the girl walked straight toward her and didn't stop until she pressed a thigh against the table and stared at Treha's food.

"That gravy looks like it's been fracked," she said. "You're actually eating that?"

Treha looked down, then back up, staring at the girl until she put down her tray and extended a hand.

"I'm Anna Waddel, and don't ever pronounce it 'waddle.' When I was in high school, the guys would quack when they called my name over the intercom. Cretins. Annaliese is my full name, but I go by Anna. What's your name?"

"Treha."

"So that's how you say it. I heard somebody say it was *Tree-ha* and thought nobody would be that cruel. How do you spell it again?"

Treha told her, thinking she could count on one hand the number of times someone had been interested enough to inquire about the correct spelling of her name.

"I've never heard that name. It's beautiful. At least the way you pronounce it. Is it French? Or Jewish, maybe? But it sounds French."

Treha shook her head and Anna sat without asking permission, all in one fell swoop as she continued talking. She arranged her salad plate and picked up a fork. "I have the metabolism of . . . whatever animal doesn't have a good metabolism. Does a hippo have bad metabolism, say, compared to a squirrel? Or an elephant?" She took a bite and sunflower seeds fell on the tray. When she could speak again, she said, "See that girl over there? The skinny one with the long legs? I've seen her drinking nacho cheese sauce with a straw. Seriously, I know, I roomed with her last year. I eat a head of lettuce spread out over a week and gain five pounds. It makes no sense to be vegan when you pork up with celery, but I guess if I ate steak and potatoes, you'd have to roll me to chapel."

Treha stared.

"Did you used to be fat? You look like someone who used to be heavy."

Treha didn't respond because she didn't know what to say.

"I don't mean anything bad by it. You look great. And if I say something that makes you mad, tell me and I'll stop. I'm told I'm way too honest. But you just look like someone who used to carry around a lot more weight."

"How can you tell?"

"I don't know, maybe the eyes give it away. Heavy people have the saddest eyes, don't you think? Like there's somebody inside waiting to unzip and step out. But they can't grab the top of the zipper. Or maybe it broke. That's how I feel. And when you do lose weight, which I've done by the way, the eyes stay the same because you can take away pockets of fat but the eyes are the window to the cellulite."

"How did you gain it back?"

"Too much lettuce, I guess. And potato salad and cheeseburgers."

"I've lost weight in the last year. About thirty pounds."

"Lucky you. How'd you do it? A pill? Exercise? I'd rather take a pill to lose weight than run five miles a day. But nobody thinks about that when they're eating an extra bag of chips. It's just a handful of this and a handful of that and pretty soon you're driving by LA Fitness with ten pounds of guilt."

Treha pushed her food with her fork. "It was a combination of things."

"Where are you from?"

"Arizona."

"That explains it. All that sunshine and being outdoors. I'd love to live in Arizona. My mother says that's my problem. I would love to live anyplace other than where I am at the moment."

"It's hot in the summer. You can't really go outside."

"But it's a dry heat, right?"

"A blast furnace is a dry heat." She'd heard Charlie say that a million times.

Anna laughed. "So how did you get your name? Is it something passed down in your family?"

"It's a long story."

"I have a lot of salad left."

"It's not a family name. It's something my mother made up."

"Sounds like you have a creative mother."

Treha didn't answer. She took a bite of cold mashed potatoes instead and hoped Anna didn't ask more questions.

Anna wiped salad dressing from her mouth. "I've seen you around. Your RA told me to talk to you but I didn't want to because I don't do well with authority. I suppose I picked the wrong school because they have a lot of rules here. Have you read the handbook?"

Treha nodded. "Why do you go here if you don't like the rules?"

Anna sighed. "My parents went here. This was their dream and it's their money, so I'm making the most of it."

"You don't believe in God?"

"No, I do. I just feel like a fish out of water at times. The only thing that keeps me going is my dream."

"Your dream?"

"Well, I have several. Like a progressive dinner. You get to one and then go on to the next course. Number one, getting out and starting my life. Dream number two, becoming a journalist. That's what I want more than anything. I've asked God to help me change the world one article at a time. Stop sex trafficking. Stop world hunger. Global warming. Justice for the downtrodden. Eradicating trans fats and GMOs."

"Is that all?"

"One more. I meet a tall, dark, hot, handsome guy who sweeps me off my feet and makes me not care about trans fats. And with hips like these, he'll have to have some upper body strength to do any sweeping." She took another bite of salad and crunched the lettuce and broccoli. “Look, I’m not usually this cynical. Well, I am, but I usually stifle it this early in a friendship.”

Treha nodded.

“You’re not real talkative, are you?”

Treha shook her head.

“That’s okay. I can hold up both ends for a while.”

A group passed, unloading their trays and tossing trash. One was Treha’s roommate, Shelly, who glanced at her and then said something to the others before they exited.

“Shelly’s a piece of work,” Anna said. “What happened with her?”

“I think she thought she was supposed to be with another roommate. She called me a freak.”

“To your face?”

“No, I heard her say it down the hall, to the RA.”

“Brutal. Doesn’t surprise me. She’s never lived on the island of misfit students. That’s why we have to stick together. Strength in numbers.”

“There’s only two of us.”

“ ‘Where two or three are gathered,’ right? It’s a start. And I know my way around. I can tell you every class to take, the best professors, the ones to avoid. Who’s your adviser?”

"Dr. Beckwith."

"English major?" Anna said.

Treha nodded.

"She's a good teacher. She cares about the material, cares about students. How are you going to use your English degree? You know, after you graduate."

Treha shrugged. "I don't know yet. I just know I like to read."

"Good. But do you want to teach? Become a writer? There must be something."

"That's what I've come here to find out."

Anna put her fork down and pushed her plate away. "Okay, I get it. Talk with Dr. Beckwith. She'll give you good direction." She handed Treha a business card she had clearly made herself. "You should consider writing for the school newspaper, the *Tower.*"

"Why is it called that?"

"The founder's great-grandfather or somebody way back built a church here and named it Bethesda, for the biblical town. It means 'house of mercy.' The bell tower in the church was used during the Civil War to spot Union soldiers coming over the ridge. They saved the tower and worked it into the construction of a new church back in the early 1900s. The architect was the same guy who designed the Ryman in Nashville.

You're looking all glazed over now, am I losing you?"

"Go ahead."

"That church became the chapel and they built the administrative wing onto it and made it the anchor for the whole school. . . . You're on overload with the new information, right? Let's make a list of questions, things you don't know, things you need to know. Like employment. Do you have a job yet?"

"No."

"I can show you where to apply. Have any work experience?"

"I've worked as a janitor."

"Perfect. If you know how to clean and aren't afraid to work in the evening, you can get hired."

Treha nodded and looked down at her food, feeling something stir in her stomach that might have been hope.

CHAPTER 4

Paige

"We polished off the cherry pie, but there's still blueberry delight and chocolate mint cake in the kitchen," I announced to the group in my living room. "And I don't want the temptation in my refrigerator all weekend."

I had made a fire in the pit outside but a slight chill in the air forced us in for dessert and wine on the leather couch and love seat and scattered chairs. My home is an oasis of books and candles and hardwood floors. The Harpeth River meanders through the countryside nearby and I find solace in the used kayak I purchased that lets me drift downstream.

Six women attended our inaugural fall meeting, though it wasn't officially fall yet. Begun as a book club by Dr. Beverly Beckwith, my mentor at Bethesda when I was a student, the group's structure had loosened over the years but stayed true to the love of writing and literature it was founded on.

Beverly was the only other English professor in the group. Ginny Baylor had brought the oldest member, Esther Richards, a woman from her church who had never been to college, let alone taught. Madalyn Palmer was there too, along with one other friend, all of us joined by a common bond with words and the warm feeling of a community. This band of women gave me a mooring, an anchor.

I sat on a sheepskin rug in front of the blackened fireplace, aged with smoke and ash. Mozart was on low in the background, another staple of the evening. Yellow firelight danced across varnished beams and hardwood.

Our official agenda dictated that each person read something from a chosen poet or novelist. Tonight I'd read a selection from Proust. Esther was up next. Sipping tea, she opened a hymnal that was falling apart and slowly worked her way through the reading of all five verses of "And Can It Be," stopping to punctuate a phrase or accentuate a word. Her crackly voice filled the room, finishing with " 'Bold I approach th' eternal throne, and claim the crown, through Christ my own.' "

A weight of silence followed and Ginny smiled broadly. "I want everyone to remember I was the one who invited her."

"That was beautiful," Beverly said.

As the praise continued for Esther's choice, I went to the kitchen to refill a couple of wineglasses. I came back to hear Beverly saying, "Based on her testing, she's off the charts intellectually, but socially awkward. And there seems to be so much going on beneath the surface."

"Speech 101 will help her come out of her shell," Ginny said. "That's how it happened with me. Showed me I had something to say."

I handed Ginny her glass. "Who are we talking about?"

"One of Beverly's new students," Ginny said.

Beverly frowned. "I don't think it's a matter of priming the pump. It's deeper. I'm her adviser, and in our first meeting . . . I can't find the combination to the lock. I can't draw her out."

"Well, if anyone can, it's you," I said.

"What's her name?" Madalyn said.

"Treha Langsam. She's from Arizona."

My heart kept beating, I'm sure of it, and I was still breathing, still seeing, though my hearing went down and all I could sense were my fingertips and the stabbing, aching pain inside my skull that had begun as soon as I heard the name *Treha.*

"That's such an interesting name," Esther said. "I've never heard that before. Is she Eastern European?"

No, I thought.

"I'm not sure she knows," Beverly said. "I helped her choose her classes — actually, I worked with someone she knows in Arizona to choose them. Paige, I had her sign up for your evening writing class."

I nearly dropped my glass of wine. Nearly choked.

"I didn't know you were teaching at Bethesda," Ginny said.

"We corralled her through the extension department," Beverly said. "It's one class, the camel nose under the tent. We hope."

I put down my glass and headed toward the kitchen again.

"Is something wrong, Paige?" Beverly said.

"No, I just need to visit the little girls' room," I said.

I stumbled into the back bathroom and locked the door. The room spun and suddenly I felt untethered, unhinged, unglued. This couldn't be. Had she found me? Had someone helped her uncover the truth about my identity? Found me in Tennessee?

This couldn't happen by chance. Was God punishing me?

For two decades I had lived with the hope or illusion that she was better off not knowing her origin, better off loving her adoptive parents. But the truth about her life, depicted in the documentary I had seen, had been a cruel revelation. She had not thrived; she had been abandoned again. She had withered like a weed, but even weeds grow through cracks in the concrete. That's what I told myself to assuage my guilt.

After seeing the film that featured Treha, I had considered flying to Arizona, finding her and explaining my choices and why I hadn't reached out to her. But no matter how tightly I wrapped myself in sheets in the dead of night, tossing and turning, I couldn't push the button to buy the plane ticket. I couldn't say yes to her. And days had turned into weeks and then months, as if looking away from a bill that had come due could make it go away.

Now, in some cosmic act of God or coincidence, the girl had returned to me.

Who was I kidding? There is no coincidence. There is punishment, retribution. Or perhaps love and mercy and grace. Which was it?

I finally made my way back to the group

and sat, numb, as their words filled the room and Mozart continued softly in the background.

"You got awfully quiet," Madalyn said at the sink later. It was eleven thirty, and she had dried and stacked the dishes I had dutifully washed.

"Just taking it all in," I said.

She smiled and hugged me; then I watched her taillights disappear down the gravel driveway. I tossed the empty bottles and hung the wineglasses and turned off the lights but let the music continue. Through the trees were stars, light from a distance, ambassadors of another galaxy, untouchable, yet still seen. Why would God allow us to see something we can't touch?

I couldn't change clothes, couldn't brush my teeth. I could only look in the mirror at my skin in harsh light, at wrinkles and creeping gray. The color tide was turning, and not in my favor. My eyes were red-veined and tired.

In the top drawer of my dresser I found the ticket stub from the documentary and stared at it. I slid to the floor, grabbed my reading light, and focused the beam on a layer of impossible dust under the bed. Wedged underneath a quilt and wrapped in a plastic bag was an aged shoe box. It had housed a pair of boots I bought shortly after returning to the US. Those had been tossed long ago, or given to Goodwill, but the box survived. I untied the shoelace that secured it and removed the top. Inside, two rubber bands held a manuscript together, a flailing attempt I had made to put my life on safe pages to squirrel away. The paper was yellowed and thick, with perforation marks at the side. The letters were small, just individual dots that made each letter whole. The printer had been an Epson, an old dot matrix.

Under the manuscript was a journal, given to me by the counselor provided by my parents' mission.

I leafed through the pages, moving past the painful trip back to the States and the lonely feelings that leaked, page after page. Emotion and questions, screaming with my pen. The depression had gotten so bad that I had gone to a doctor — again, provided by the mission.

> Dr. Crenshaw gave me medication today. He said I wouldn't have to pay, that it was experimental, and it wouldn't hurt the baby. I signed the document. I just want to feel better and not so alone with all of this.

That same doctor had showed up on the documentary, had revealed a puzzle piece to Treha's life, and had shown me reasons why I had trouble trusting authority figures.

I placed the journal in the box and put the ticket stub on top, then covered it and slid it back to its rightful place.

There is no greater power on earth than a mother's love, unless it is a mother's guilt.

CHAPTER 5

Treha

Monday was the longest day of the week for Treha. She had morning classes and worked in the afternoon. Then she just had time to grab something for dinner before her evening class started. Treha loved schedules, loved the flow of the day, but she hated hurrying and her empty stomach made it worse.

She'd just settled into a booth in the commons when her cell phone vibrated. She could count on one hand the times that had happened, in comparison with other students who seemed to constantly be on the phone.

"You're not in class or anything, are you?" Miriam said. "Is this a good time?"

"This is good."

"I've tried to hold back from calling. You can ask Charlie, it nearly kills me. But I love your e-mails and the pictures of the campus are gorgeous."

"I've never been around so many trees."

"I imagine there's a lot different there. How are classes?"

"Okay. Tell me about Charlie."

"Charlie is a rascal. He's driving me to work every day and picking me up. And he's latched on to this book we're going through together on marriage."

"Does he still listen to talk radio?"

"Of course. He's trying to keep me informed on all the political shenanigans."

"That sounds like a word he would use."

Anna plopped down across from Treha and immediately began texting and eating yogurt with a plastic spoon. Treha covered one ear and turned away to concentrate.

"He talks about you all the time, Treha. And Elsie and I get together and compare notes on your e-mails. That woman is praying for you constantly. I hope you know that."

Treha touched her phone as if she were reaching through to Miriam.

"How's the roommate situation?"

Treha wanted to tell Miriam how hard it was with Shelly and a hundred other things that flashed through her mind, images and feelings coming alive because she was alone in a strange place and only had her journal. And Anna. "It's okay. I try to stay out of her way."

"Good for you. I'm glad you're making the best of it. Sometimes the biggest lessons in life are learned outside the classroom."

"I got a job."

"You what?" Miriam couldn't hide her excitement. "That's great, Treha. Doing what?"

"I'm doing the same thing I did at Desert Gardens. I'm on the cleaning crew. It's not much but —"

"No, that's wonderful! I wish we could have given enough that you didn't have to work for some extra spending money."

"It keeps me busy and my mind occupied."

"I'm so happy for you. I can't wait to tell Elsie." After a moment of silence, Miriam said, "It's so good to hear your voice. I just wanted to hear you. And let you know I pray for you every day. And I meet Elsie at breakfast and we storm the gates of heaven for you and all the students."

Anna paused her furious texting and looked up at Treha.

"I think I'd better go," Treha said.

"All right, dear. Just wanted you to know how much I'm thinking about you." There was a smile in the woman's voice. "Love you, Treha."

She clicked the End button.

"Somebody from Arizona?" Anna said.

Treha nodded.

"The lady who took you in?"

"She and her husband did." Treha put her phone away.

"They sound like nice people." Anna got another text and as she answered it, she took another bite of yogurt and ate as she talked. "Probably want you to come back there over the Christmas break. Do you have plans for Thanksgiving?"

Treha shook her head.

"You can stay at my dad's house with me. I usually go there for Thanksgiving and then to my mom's for Black Friday and the rest of the weekend. It feels like it's a long way away, with school barely started, but it's really not. It'll go fast."

"Your parents are divorced?"

"Yeah. My mom learned a hard lesson. Don't pick the first guy that makes your heart flutter. That's what she did. They were on the same page early on, going to change the world and all that. Then one day Mom said she woke up alone. And Dad was still there. He had a midlife crisis and needed to 'find himself' and said stuff like 'This is not your fault. This is about me.' It was brutal. He finally went off the deep end. Found a group of guys and went howling into the woods. No, seriously, they literally went into the woods and howled."

"But you wouldn't be here if they hadn't gotten married."

"Yes, and the world would be such a darker place, wouldn't it?" Anna gave a wry smile.

Treha looked at the clock. "I have to go. I have a class tonight."

"What class?"

"Reading and Composition. Dr. Beckwith said I should take it."

"Huh. Who's the prof?"

"Someone named Ms. Redwine."

CHAPTER 6

Paige

For more than twenty years I had waited for my daughter to walk through the classroom door of my life. Proverbially. And now it was going to happen. The anticipation wrapped around my soul like a three-stranded cord of longing, dread, and angst.

I arrived early on the Bethesda campus and sat in the commons to see if I could catch a glimpse of her. Twice I thought I saw her. In the film her face had been blurred, so I had to imagine. The friends and laughter and good-natured conversation were things I prayed my daughter might experience. The vision of them talking and having a "normal" life gave me hope that maybe Treha had improved and put the past behind her.

There was, of course, the possibility this was what I wanted for myself. If I could see her functioning well . . . if I could watch from a distance and know that she had turned out all right despite my mistakes, I could go on with life. Since learning that Treha would be in my class, I had considered every permutation to avoid her. I could drop the assignment and rightfully say I was too busy. Beverly would understand. Instead I allowed time and my own indecision to make the decision for me.

As I was leaving the commons, someone called my name. I turned and the Bethesda tower was framed in the background along with a stately oak tree in full bloom — the perfect picture.

"I was hoping I'd run into you," Ron Gleason said, smiling. "How does it feel to be back on campus?"

I was taken off guard and had to think quickly, which is not my strength. "It's . . . interesting. A little scary, but good. How are you?"

"Fine. Great. Can I carry that to class for you?"

He reached for my computer bag but I didn't offer it. "I'm fine, Ron. But thank you. Trying to get my game face on for the lecture."

"I understand."

"I've been through the material many times but coming back here is kind of unbalancing. Some things I have to work through."

He nodded. "I'll be praying."

"Thank you."

Then came the awkward silence, the moment when I had to choose whether I would take care of him or myself, and I took a step backward, toward the academic hall.

"This is probably not the best time, but have you thought more about what we talked about?" he said.

I stopped, but my heart didn't. Its pace increased. "I have. . . ." I like speeches much better when they're written down. There is no teleprompter for the heart, no script for this conversation, and I could see in his eyes that he knew. "Let me call you, and maybe we can grab coffee?"

"Yeah, I'd like that," he said, smiling again, a little sadly this time. "Don't let me hold you up. It's always good seeing you."

I walked away with another five pounds of guilt added to the already-unmanageable pack I felt on my shoulders.

I set up at the desk in front of the room, plugged in my computer with a shaking hand, and made small talk with students who had already assembled. But I couldn't find her. Her name was on the list but I couldn't pick her out.

Then my injured child entered. It was like watching a lost piece of myself walk into the room. All the counseling I'd been through, all the journaling and sleepless nights and questions and tears, coalesced into a single moment when she walked through the door. Her untied shoelaces clicked on the floor. She walked head down, brown hair covering her face. She skittered behind me and searched for a seat and finally settled.

I had to fight to keep from staring. I wanted to know if she had my ears, my eyes, my nose — anything of me. Part of me wanted to step in front of her desk and tell her everything. That I was her mother, that I hadn't abandoned her but released her to what I thought would be a better life. That I was sorry. That I needed her to forgive me.

Instead, I moved forward and lost myself in the carefully crafted opening to the class, a short devotional followed by a review of the syllabus. Then I came to the hardest part. Never had calling the roll caused such an internal storm.

"Drenna Adkins?"

"Here."

"Melanie Bailey?"

"Here."

There were twenty-three students in the class, and the *L*s began at number thirteen.

If I were superstitious, that would have bothered me.

"Treha Langsam?"

"Yes," she said.

Her voice sent a shiver through me. In the moments after birth, she'd given a cry of pain I've never gotten out of my head. When I hear a baby wailing in a mall or in church, I think of her. School buses pass and I wonder where she might be. What did her first-grade teacher say about her? Did she play with Barbies? Did she love stories as much as I did? Did she ever learn an instrument? Did she need braces?

I kept my head down and called the rest of the names.

After the roll I clicked through quotations that flashed on the screen behind me.

"We write to discover what we think." Joan Didion.

The next was from Daniel Boorstin and brought chuckles. *"I write to discover what I think. After all, the bars aren't open that early."*

The final quote was my favorite. *"I write because I don't know what I think until I read what I say." Flannery O'Connor.*

Several students gave thoughtful *hmmm* sounds.

"I don't want to shatter any illusions, but here is the truth," I said. "Writing is pain. I will teach you that."

Scattered nervous laughter around the room.

"Writing is joy, as well. Writing is learning and discovery. If you let it, writing will change you."

I tried to keep from looking at Treha, but I couldn't help glancing at her. Just a peek into the window of her soul.

"In this class, we'll be using the two tools at a writer's disposal: writing and reading. There is no substitute for these. You will read and learn, and you will write and discover."

I gave a reading assignment for next week's class, then handed out folded pieces of paper, making sure I gave Treha's row the correct writing prompt.

"This is a good first exercise. I want to take away some of the fear you have of getting things wrong. This class is not about writing perfectly. I want you to see how rough your first draft can be and still be good. For the rest of the class — we have twenty minutes or so — I'd like you to open the page and look at the prompt on it. Whatever comes to your mind, the first thing that jumps to the surface, I'd like you to follow that. If you want to write longhand, you can do that. If you want to use your computer, my e-mail address is at the bottom of the page, but leave what you write with me or send it to me before you leave. Don't think. Write what comes into your head. Don't go back and cross things out. Let it spill."

I put on some atmospheric music, a sound track by Thomas Newman. As heads went down in contemplation, I sat at the desk and gathered my materials, but I couldn't keep my eyes from straying to Treha. She struggled, bit at her thumbnail, picked up the page and studied the words and put the paper down again, wrote in a spiral notebook, then ripped the sheet out loudly, looked around her apologetically, and lowered her head again.

What's good for the goose, I thought, *is good for the teacher,* so I opened a notebook of my own. I used one of the prompts I'd given my students.

The most pain I've ever felt . . .

The most pain I've ever felt happened in a delivery room at a hospital I cannot recall. Searing pain I thought would tear me apart. It made me tremble inside and the exhaustion washed over me like a river. I gritted my teeth and promised I would not scream, would not let the pain overtake me. I would control it. I clawed at the sheets and the metal handles of the bed and vowed this would not undo me.

The pain in my body could not match the pain her cry surfaced in my heart. They cleaned her, weighed her, wrapped her, and whisked her away. And it was then that I realized the much-greater pain is not in giving birth but in releasing your own child.

I looked up at the students standing in front of my desk. Trancelike, I had written furiously and hadn't seen them waiting to give me their papers. The feeling surprised me and I apologized. Why couldn't I write my dissertation like this?

When I looked for my daughter, her seat was empty. While a few students kept writing, I riffled through the pages in front of me and found one torn from a notebook, the edge still ragged. My eyes traced the letters of her name at the top. I had given her this name, an anagram for the word *heart* — something unique that would allow me to find her one day even though the adoption was private.

The thing I want in life that I've never had is a roommate who doesn't . . .

This had been struck through, and three lines down, the scrawl started again.

The thing I want in life that I've never had is to know my mother. I was given up for adoption at birth and I've looked for her. But I can't find her and I don't think I want to find her anymore because if I was supposed to find her, it would have happened. Maybe God doesn't want me to find her. Maybe he is telling me that I don't have to know her in order to go on with my life. I wanted all my questions answered and everything wrapped and tied with a bow. But life is not neat bows and nice packages. Life is messy and you don't get all your questions answered.

I have never had a boyfriend. I have never had a dog or a cat or a pet of any kind. I have never had a real home. I can list a million things I've never had. But I have a mother and don't know her and I've . . .

I don't think this is what you were looking for, but this is the first thing that came to my mind, so I wrote it down.

I gathered the pages in a stack and put them away and waited for the last students to finish. Then I went to my car and drove the long road home, pulling over twice because I couldn't see.

CHAPTER 7

Treha

Treha sat on the right side of the auditorium for chapel, about two-thirds of the way back, in the middle of the row, and opened the hymnal. She recognized a few songs that Elsie, her elderly friend in Arizona, had taught her. "A Mighty Fortress Is Our God." "All Hail the Power of Jesus' Name." "Amazing Grace." "Holy, Holy, Holy." And Elsie's favorite, "Great Is Thy Faithfulness." Elsie believed singing hymns was a lost art. When they sat together at Desert Gardens, she would take Treha line by line and teach her theology with the words.

> When I survey the wondrous cross
> On which the Prince of glory died,
> My richest gain I count but loss,
> And pour contempt on all my pride.

Elsie had spent half an hour on that verse,

telling Treha it was the cross of Jesus, his substitution, his atonement, that brought forgiveness. Then she'd taken her to the Old Testament sacrificial system and explained that this gift of God's own Son was for her.

Treha believed Elsie was right about all of this. She had no problem believing in God. Her only question was how she fit into the divine plan and if God cared for orphan girls.

The old woman's words echoed in Treha's mind as students filled the rows of the chapel. In the row directly in front of her, she saw Cameron squeeze past his friends. Cameron Goodman. Others called him "Cam." Treha had noticed this when she first saw him at orientation. He was tall with dark, curly hair. She'd heard girls talking about him — how nice he was. How he had helped them study.

The others raised their knees so he couldn't get by, which she thought was mean, but Cameron laughed as if he enjoyed moving through the gauntlet. He was strong, athletic, confident.

He pushed his seat down and looked at Treha. Every time she had seen him, he'd been smiling. In the hall, at lunch, holding a door for people. He didn't break the string when he said, "Hi."

Treha evaluated a person by their first words, by the kindness or stress or preoccupation in their voice. The words themselves or something in between the lines. With Cameron, she felt more. Warmth. Vulnerability. He didn't try to hide his acne scars and she liked that. His eyes crinkled when he smiled and dimples appeared in his cheeks and she thought he was the cutest thing she had ever seen.

Her response was a nod. No words. No, "Hello, how are you?" Just an uncomfortable nod that he smiled at, then turned around. If others judged her by first words or impressions, she would fail the test each time.

Anna slipped in beside Treha and patted her on the shoulder. "Cute, isn't he?" she whispered.

Treha didn't respond except to feel herself turn beet red. She stood when told to stand but didn't sing. She didn't want to embarrass herself or let certain people hear her singing off-key. But she did follow the words and mouth them.

"Do you have a class now?" Anna said when the service was over.

Treha didn't.

"Good. Then you can help me with my assignment."

Treha was distracted because Cameron was getting up and she wanted to say something to him but wasn't sure what. Something more than a nod.

"Bye, Treha," Cameron said.

Too stunned to speak. He knew her name. And the way he said it. So familiar. So casual. So . . . nice.

"Whoa," Anna said. "That looked like a real connection there. Why didn't you talk to him?"

Treha shrugged but on the inside, she was kicking herself.

"It was sort of a warm wave you gave him, though."

"What did you want me to help you with?"

"An article for the *Tower.* All you have to do is answer a few questions." Anna opened her notebook to a blank page. "I'm highlighting new students and their backgrounds, hopes, dreams, and all that. I pitched this series idea on new students, and the editor bit and now I'm on deadline. First issue comes out Thursday. You'd help me a lot."

Treha watched Cameron walk to the back of the auditorium and linger with friends. Smiling. Talking.

"I don't want to be in the paper," Treha said.

Anna looked stunned. "Everybody's looking for their fifteen minutes of fame. You'd have your picture in there and everything. It'd be great exposure."

"I don't want exposure. I've had that."

"What do you mean?"

Treha didn't answer, but she was thinking of the documentary. The film had won acclaim, and several women had come forward claiming to be Treha's mother, but none of them were. The truth was, Treha had never seen the film all the way through, only bits and pieces, and she didn't want to see it. She wanted to forget so much.

Anna scratched her head. "Well, I guess that means I can't help you with Cameron."

"Help me?"

Anna smiled. "I know him. I could introduce you. Like, formally. Maybe even get you a date. But you'll need to let me write the article."

"I don't want my picture taken."

"Okay. . . . Hey, that's a good hook. Anonymous conversations with new students. Total honesty. I like it."

Treha looked over her shoulder as Cameron finally left the auditorium.

"He's from a little town in Pennsylvania, near Gettysburg," Anna said. "Speaks English and fluent Spanish and Portuguese because his parents served in Africa or someplace where they speak two languages."

"You're friends with him?"

"Not exactly. That was on his Facebook page."

"You're friends with him on Facebook?"

"Not exactly. I just looked around from a friend's account who is — now don't look at me like that. You can learn a lot about a person there. Cameron plays the guitar, sings, and doesn't believe the gift of tongues is for today. Amillennial in his eschatology. Leans toward Calvinism, eternal security and total depravity."

"I don't know what you're talking about."

"That was my problem too. I didn't really know what they were talking about, but you will if you make friends with Cameron. I sat next to him in the lunchroom a few times last year. Well, not next to him, just kind of behind him and off to the side where I could hear. He talked about theology and church discipline and whether we're losing our moorings from a bibliocentric worldview and it made my head hurt. Though it could have been the shepherd's pie they served that day. They use way too much salt in the cafeteria."

"I don't think I'll ever fit in here."

"Sure you will, Treha. But you have to

take a step toward other people. You have to risk. And a good step might be this article. Come on, it's a few innocuous questions. It'll be painless."

Treha thought for a moment. She wasn't interested at all in publicity or being "out there." She wanted anonymity and to be left alone. But maybe Anna was right.

"Would you really help me get to know him?"

"Sure. Let's go to the commons and I'll ask you the questions."

Chapter 8

Paige

I drove up Beverly Beckwith's long, winding driveway, gravel crunching under the tires. Three other homes shared the driveway, but Beverly's place was at the top, overlooking Thompson's Station. Beverly's husband had passed away prematurely of heart disease several years earlier, and though people had tried to get her to move closer to civilization, the woman wouldn't. The first time I came here, I'd been a student, straight out of the jungles of New Guinea. The peaceful surroundings, the cattle, the trees, the ponds and creeks brought back good memories.

Beverly's elderly dog wagged his tail on the front porch and thought about barking, then took a breath and put his head back on the weathered wood and fell asleep.

"Paige Redwine!" the woman said through the screen. She came outside and hugged me fiercely. "This calls for a celebration! Kill the fatted calf, my daughter has come home!"

"Let the fatted calf live until you get a bigger crowd," I said.

She laughed. "Then we'll make do with gingersnaps. Come on in."

"Would you mind if we sat out here? It's so beautiful."

Beverly brought the bag of ancient cookies and put it between us on the porch swing. A light breeze wafted through the valley and there was a hint of rain, a hint of fall.

"Can I get you something to drink?"

I shook my head and patted Beverly's thin leg. "Just sit with me."

A smile and a little silence. That's all it took to get us back to the beginning, back to each other's hearts.

"Tell me about your class," she said. "Are you enjoying teaching at Bethesda?"

"Being back is strange. But it's good to spread my wings. They're bright students." I paused, then admitted, "Dr. Waldron gave me an ultimatum about my thesis."

"Is that the reason for the pensive look?"

"That's part of it."

"Your writing not going well?"

"My writing is a *dry* well."

"But there's something else lurking behind that pretty face of yours, isn't there?"

Deep breath. I stared at my hands. At a scar from a boil my father lanced when I was a child. He pushed and poked so hard, the pain incredible. "I need some advice."

"About what?"

"The past."

"Ahh. Well, as you know, I've never held back my opinions from you. So if it's advice you need . . ."

"I thought I had worked it through. I thought I was immune."

"From the past? My dear, even if you deal with it well, the past boomerangs. And God has this funny way of stretching and changing and pushing us toward things we don't want to face. I don't think the past is something we deal with as much as it deals with us."

She put a hand down by her side and stroked the back of the motionless dog, who batted rheumy eyes, then closed them. "The alternative to life, to living fully, is not death, it's suppression. It's building a dam on a steady river ready to rush over the rocks and carve out a Grand Canyon. Debris holds the water back. It blocks the whole thing."

"And that's how I feel. Blocked. Stuck."

"Why?"

"I don't know."

Beverly dipped her head and gave me the look. I had transgressed her law, my own law. Neither of us allowed students to use those words. I pulled both feet under me on the swing, the silence unnerving me.

She reached out with a foot and pushed the swing gently into motion, the two of us moving at her command. "My theory is simple," she said finally. "You can live under the weight of your past or the weight of forgiveness. If you choose the former, you'll constantly be working off the guilt like someone who overeats at the holidays."

"I don't understand why I can't be over all this. I don't see why it's taking so long. It's been more than twenty years."

"Twenty years ago. Let's start there. When you first came to the school, you were scared. Scarred. A little wounded."

"A lot wounded."

"Okay, a lot. We had good talks. You blossomed. You've come a long way and I'm proud of what you've accomplished."

"But . . . ?"

When she chuckled, the folds of skin on her neck jiggled, then contracted as she swallowed. "You like staying hidden, Paige. Your essays, early on, were always about someone else. Your parents. The tribe you lived with. I had to prod you to dig into your own heart, and it was like a shovel on rock. It still is, isn't it?"

"Either that or concrete." A thought streaked across my brain like a meteor and I spoke it after the trail flamed out. "You've talked with Ron, haven't you?"

She laughed. "Ron Gleason? Now there's a wonderful man. You should give him more consideration."

"He's short."

"Ron has the heart of a lion and an intact spine, unlike a lot of men. He cares about you, Paige. But he didn't ask me to intercede. He's asked questions about you, asked for general advice, and I gave it."

"What advice?"

"Not to push you. To be patient. Change is something that comes hard for you."

"Thank you for that."

"I'm a terrible matchmaker, but in my opinion, this is one you shouldn't let get away."

"I know he's wonderful. I just don't think I can take on a relationship."

"You mean now or ever? If the apostle Paul himself asked you out, I doubt you'd be open."

"I can't imagine what I'd wear."

She laughed, then turned serious. "Paige, you've been trifling with big themes all your life. Trying to figure out the meaning and purpose of the stories." She spread her hands across her lap. "No good story is free from death or the specter of it. And perhaps the thing you fear, the thing that's holding you back, is this possibility."

"That I'll die?"

"No. That you'll be called to really live. Not to analyze or explain or critique or grade. Not to help someone else or mentor. To put away the red pen. To pick up the black ink."

I looked at her. "The bugs are worse out here than I thought. Can we go inside?"

She gave a smile and led me to her library. She had a lifetime of collected books scattered throughout the house on shelves and stacked by walls, but her treasures, the real "keepers" as she called them, were in this room by the front door. I'd spent hours there as a student, pulling down volumes, reading notes made in the margins. And it was with all those tomes around me, breathing in the smell of the real books, that I felt something loosen.

I pulled Treha's essay from my purse and handed it to Beverly.

She scanned the page. "Remarkable, isn't

she? Rare candor from someone who's had a difficult life."

"Yes."

"I suggested she take your class — wait, I've told you that, haven't I?"

"You did." My voice sounded vacant, raspy, and hollow. I glanced behind her at the leather-bound books that lined her shelves and caught sight of *The Scarlet Letter.*

Beverly leaned forward. "Paige, what is it?"

Without hesitation, without thinking, I blurted out, "I have a child."

Saying those words was like giving birth again. My breath was short and the room felt like it was closing in. Beverly nodded and moved closer, her face right there, willing me forward, into the abyss.

"Before I came to Bethesda," I said haltingly, "right before, I got pregnant. It nearly killed my parents. They had such high hopes. I was their life. And when this happened, their world imploded. They didn't believe in abortion. But they said they were protecting me. Trying to give me a future. So they arranged a closed adoption in the States, worked through backdoor channels, a pastor they had known who knew someone else who knew a family. I went along with it. I had made such a mess of my life."

"And the problem went away."

"Right."

"But it didn't."

I shook my head and tried to hold the emotion back but it kept rising like a tide. "I thought it was best for the child. To grow up in a loving home, with people who followed God."

"But in your heart, you wanted to know your . . . son?"

"Daughter."

"Your daughter. That's wonderful, Paige."

The tears began with her words. I had lived so long thinking everything but *wonderful* about my life, my child, and to hear her say that sent me over the edge.

"You saved my life," I said through the sobs. "You know that, don't you?"

She enveloped me in a motherly hug. "God brought you here at the right time. He knew what you needed. I didn't."

"You're the reason I wanted to become a teacher. To help someone else. To give what you gave me."

Dr. Beckwith smiled through her own tears. "Your daughter. Do you know where she is?"

I picked up the paper in the woman's lap and held it out to her.

"Treha?" she said. Her mouth dropped at the revelation. "How . . . ? She must be ecstatic to finally know. How did you tell her?"

I didn't say anything. I didn't have to.

Beverly held me and swallowed hard. "Paige, you have to tell her. Unless there's part of you that's unsure."

"I know she's my daughter. I haven't done a DNA test, but there's a distinct family resemblance. And her name. It was the only thing I gave her except for her life."

"Then why haven't you told her?"

"I'm scared of what it might do. I don't want to bring her more pain."

She pulled back. "Nonsense. You don't want to bring yourself more pain."

My heart fluttered. "Honestly, I'm afraid she'll —"

"Paige, that girl has been living with a hole in her heart her entire life. Even if she had wonderful adoptive parents, there's some part of her that wonders where she came from."

"I just . . . Once that domino falls, once that choice is made, we can't go back. Ever."

Silence again. And it became increasingly hard to listen.

"What about her father?" Beverly said. "Do you know where he is?"

I nodded.

She thought a moment, her arm around my shoulder. Then a deep sigh. "I don't know where this will lead you. I don't know how people will react. I don't know how *Treha* will react. You can't control any of that. But take this a step at a time. Focus on Treha. You do what's best for her, and in the end, it will be what's best for you."

"What if she rejects me?"

"That's a risk. But what if she never has the chance to reject you or embrace you? That doesn't seem fair."

"No, it's not." My vision clouded again and the books behind her blurred. "How do I do it? How do I tell her?"

"I don't know."

"Not a good answer," I said.

"But it's the truth. I can't tell you how to do it. But I can tell you that you need to. Soon. The enemy wants you to suppress, to hide. God and your daughter are calling you to something deeper than you wanted. This is your wonderful, heartbreaking, engrossing tale."

"It's not a story."

"No. It's your life. And God is working in it, calling you to something more. So let's turn the page."

Chapter 9

Treha

On Thursday morning, when she entered the commons, Treha saw the stack of papers in what had been empty bins. Her photo stared back at her above the fold and she felt sick to her stomach. She wanted to grab all the papers and throw them in the Dumpster or cart them to her room and hide them. But the papers were everywhere. In every building. In all the newspaper bins. And full-time employees were getting them in their mailboxes. Wasn't it wrong to destroy school property?

Suddenly Treha wanted to go home, go away from this place and not return. Just run.

She sat in the booth where she studied every morning to avoid waking Shelly. There, on page 3, was her face again, bigger this time. No smile. Just looking slightly off camera. And there was her name in bold letters underneath the picture. And there were her answers to the questions Anna had posed, her story for all to see, students and faculty. Treha felt naked, exposed, as if someone had not only ripped off her clothes but pushed her onto a stage in front of everyone and turned on a bright-white spotlight. How could Anna do this? Why had she trusted her?

"Did you see the article?" Anna's voice was chipper and hopeful. She plopped down in the seat across from Treha and turned the paper to look at it. "I figured you'd be here early. I think it turned out really well, don't you?"

She handed the paper back, but Treha stared at her. "You lied to me."

Two hands up in front of her. "Whoa, hold on."

"You said you wouldn't print my picture or my name. You said I would be anonymous."

"See, that's the thing with making promises. I swear I tried to keep it. I told them at the paper that you didn't want your picture —"

"You *said* I could remain anonymous."

"I know. And that's what I thought, Treha. But the editor didn't like the idea, and I didn't know they had a rule about anonymous interviews or letters to the editor. Everything has to be attributed. And I fought them. I went to bat for you."

"You shouldn't have turned it in."

"I was on deadline. I had to."

"No, you had a choice. To keep your promise or not. You chose to do this." She put her finger on her picture.

"Look, I don't see what the big deal is. It's a great interview. You're going to have people thanking you for being so honest about school. Just wait. You'll see."

"You had no right."

"Treha, don't be obtuse."

Treha couldn't help it. All the letters of the word *obtuse* went through her mind — six letters, jumbled and rumbling through her cerebral cortex, mixing and matching and forming other words. *Best. Bust. Stub. Tube. Sub. Sob.*

"There's nothing in there that's not true. There's nothing to be ashamed of."

"How can you call me obtuse when you told me you wouldn't do what you did?"

"Let me explain. I can help you understand."

"I don't need your help. I understand." Treha gathered her things and rose from the booth.

"I thought you were my friend, Treha."

Treha looked back, her brow furrowed, wanting to say something but refraining.

With emotion, Anna said, "I thought you'd see what a bind I was in and you'd forgive me."

Treha walked outside, clutching her backpack, trying to think the best. Maybe no one would read the article. Maybe they would recycle the paper. But in her first class, three people came up to her. She walked into chapel but couldn't sit in her normal spot for fear others would approach. She climbed to the balcony and found a seat as far away from everyone as she could, but even there she was spotted and saw a young man she didn't know point at her picture.

She went back to her room before her next class because she didn't know what else to do.

Shelly was in bed, wild hair hanging over her face, but she was holding a copy of the paper. "What were you thinking?" she spat. "You don't think people will know who your roommate is?"

Treha stood frozen. Take away the makeup and perfect hair and put in a retainer and Shelly looked a lot like everyone else.

"I didn't say those things to hurt you," Treha said.

"Then why did you say them?"

Treha wanted to explain about Anna, about the promise she'd broken, but what was the point? If Shelly could read an article about Treha and only think of herself, she wouldn't listen.

"I knew this would never work out," Shelly said. "I should have stuck to my guns from the start."

Shelly stood. She wore a T-shirt and gym shorts but Treha stared at her fluffy pink socks. On her way out of the room, she turned back and said, "I swear, Treha, you're digging a hole with stuff like this. And you're already six feet down."

CHAPTER 10

Paige

When there is something you know you must do, something you are called to do that will change your life, the legions of hell will remind you to take out the trash. Things you haven't dusted in years rise up as incredibly important. Lingering bills call your name.

Finally on Saturday the phone beckoned, guilt drawing me toward what I hadn't done in weeks. I hadn't talked to my parents.

When I say I hadn't talked to *them,* I mean I hadn't talked to her. There was no *them* any longer with my father's descent into the netherworld of his own mind. The man who had pulled words from the lips of tribal men and women and placed them on pages could no longer form them himself. He listened, Mom said, when she turned on the speakerphone, but it had been several months since he had so much as grunted into the phone.

This was a conversation I knew I had to have, even before I revealed myself to Treha. If I could tell my own mother, I could tell anyone.

I dialed the first ten numbers that led from my home to theirs and hung up. It's always the eleventh number that's the hardest.

I cleaned a few more things and organized another bookshelf, but it wasn't until my mind rested on Treha that I picked up the phone and punched in the numbers, then added the 7, the final number in the sequence. The perfect number, the number of completion.

"Yes — hello?" my mother said. Sentences that are important to her or that she's anxious about begin with a *yes,* something she'd done as long as I could remember. It was both endearing and maddening. I knew she had caller ID and that my name had popped up on her display.

"Mom, it's me. How are you?"

"Oh, Paige, it's good to hear your voice again. It's been such a long time."

There was the guilt. It came in small doses if I called and larger ones if I didn't. I'd had what I would term a good relationship with my mother until the teenage years, until the emergence of the independent Paige. And when my mother discovered I was pregnant, it forever changed our relationship. Garden doors were barred and locked and I was banished to the east of my mother's Eden.

"Well, it's the start of the school year here. Things have been busy."

"Yes — I'll bet. How is everything? And the class you're teaching at Bethesda — how is it being back there?"

"It's going well, Mom. Is Dad there? Is he okay?"

"He's fine. He's just finishing his breakfast. I'll put you on the speaker."

"No, please don't. Let him eat. I just want to talk to you."

"All right. He's having his usual breakfast today. We went to the doctor yesterday. . . ."

What followed was a rundown of his diet, the physical problems he had experienced recently, and the slight change in dosage in an unending lineup of medications. I listened for a pause or a possibility for steering the conversation toward me, but settled on asking follow-ups about Dad. My mother lived a Row-Row-Row-Your-Boat round that never ended, just kept looping back to the beginning each morning. She loved him — she always had — and never complained, but I could hear in her voice the toll the past few years had taken, and it made my revelation even harder.

When she took a breath, I mustered the courage to interrupt her report. "Listen, Mom, I have something to tell you. Something's happened."

Her voice turned grave. "Oh? This sounds serious."

"Nothing bad. At least I don't think it is. In fact, I've kind of been hoping I could make this call for a long time."

"Yes — this doesn't have anything to do with that professor you've been seeing? I've heard good things about him."

"No, Mom, it's not about Ron. That's actually kind of fizzling at the moment."

"Well, I'm sorry to hear that. You know, Paige, you're not getting any younger."

The jab stung. My mother had told me for years that I simply needed to jump into the pool of eligible men. If she lived closer, I was sure she would push me in. In fact, she had given my number to friends who had single sons.

"I've come in contact with someone from the past. Someone unexpected."

"Really? From New Guinea? Someone you knew from the mission?"

"No." I took a deep breath, composed my thoughts.

"That seems like another lifetime, doesn't it? So long ago."

"Mom, I've found my daughter."

Silence on the other end. I've said that women do better with silence than men, and I still hold to that. But wordlessness is not the same as silence. Other, stronger daughters might have been able to resist filling in the gaps of my mother's stone-coldness, but not me.

"I actually found out about her some time ago. Through a strange twist, our paths have crossed —"

"Why would you want to hurt us like this?"

The tone of her voice took me back twenty years. The smell of the earthen floor, the thatched roof, the sweat and heat and fecund aroma of untethered goats. The taste of warm milk. The woodsmoke. The cluck of chickens and laughter of children and the unraveling of my life. Whispered words through blankets draped for walls. She hadn't wept. No wails or keening. Maybe that unnerved me more than if she'd had a breakdown.

"Why on earth would you go looking for her? Why would you intentionally drag us through this muck again?"

"I didn't go looking for her. And there's

no part of this that I'm doing to hurt you. This is not about you."

"It's about all of us, Paige." She lowered her voice and it sounded like she was moving around in the house. "You can't separate any of us from it."

"Mom, I've thought of her every day. I've wondered what happened. I've prayed for her. Surely you've done the same."

"Of course I have, but I would never drag her into my life when that's not the best thing."

"She wants to know her mother. She wants a relationship with me."

"How could you possibly know that?"

"It's a long story."

"Yes — I'm sure it is, and it's going to get longer and more painful if you do this. I'm begging you, Paige. Nothing good can come from this."

"And what if God is the one who is drawing us? What if he is the one who brought her to me?"

"Don't blame God for your mistake."

I felt my jaw clench. "I'm *not* blaming him. I'm saying this whole thing has to be something he's orchestrating. I found out about her last year. I left her alone. I wanted to pick up the phone or hop on a plane, but I didn't have the strength. But now she's in my life, through no finagling. She's my *student,* Mom. I have to tell her."

"You can't be sure of that. It's probably a mistake."

"No, it's no mistake. It's her."

"Paige, don't you see what this will do to us." It was a statement, not a question. An indictment. "This will kill your father."

"How? He doesn't recognize me. He can't speak. How will it kill him?"

"You made a promise."

"I was a child. I felt guilty. And I wanted you to forgive me."

More silence on the line.

"We've never really talked through this, Mom. Dad and I had a couple good conversations before I came to the States. He helped me see that my life didn't have to end because of a mistake. I'll always love him for that."

"And what did you get from me? Condemnation? I did nothing but love you and hope for the best. And you promised you would close this door and leave it closed."

"It was a foolish promise."

"It was the right thing. The kind thing. This girl probably has her own life, with her own parents. Can you imagine the shock this is going to be if she doesn't even know she was adopted?"

"She knows. But the adoption didn't turn out the way —"

"And what's to keep her from coming to us for support?" she said, interrupting. "We're barely making it, Paige. And you're not in any position to help financially. This is going to cost so much time and energy and finances and emotion. Don't rush into it. Think through the ramifications. You could make a hasty decision you'll regret for years."

"I made a decision I have regretted every day."

"Placing her for adoption? Is that what you mean? You were a child; how would you have cared for a baby?"

"That's not the point."

"Then what is the point? What are you accomplishing other than bringing more pain?"

"I know it will be painful, Mom. Why can't you trust me?"

"I did trust you. That's how we got into this mess."

Cruel. That was the only way to describe it. I've always heard that people in pain lash out. But there was something else, a different fear I couldn't pinpoint behind her words.

"I guess I'll have to move forward without

your blessing."

"Is that why you called? To receive my blessing?"

"I was hoping you would support me, even if you thought it a bad idea. Something like 'I don't agree, but I'm here for you.' Maybe that's too much to ask."

"Of course I'm here for you. That's why I'm asking you to reconsider."

"It's not fair to her to keep hidden. She deserves to know."

More silence. The machines turning, the inner translator interpreting the words, the history between us, the pain.

"When she asks, what are you going to tell her about her father? You know she'll have that question, Paige."

She said my name like it was a four-letter word. I wanted to hang up. I wanted to jump in the time machine and go back to the second before I dialed the 7. The second before I signed the paper to place my child in a stranger's arms. The second before I first met *him.*

I put a hand to my temple and pressed on the beginnings of a migraine. "I'm sure you're right. She's going to ask. And I'll simply tell her the truth."

"Listen to yourself. You're stepping into something that's way over your head. You have enough on your plate with your dissertation and your classes — to add this doesn't make sense. Press forward. Move on."

"Mom?" I said it to get her to stop. I said it as a plea — something almost like a prayer. "What do you think Dad would say?"

Another long pause. "We'll never know, will we?"

Chapter 11

Treha

Anna's voice rang down the hall as Treha walked resolutely away. "Please stop. I have something important to say."

Treha stopped near the stairwell of her dorm but didn't look at the girl. Couldn't look at her.

"I know you're still ticked off. I understand. You were right. I shouldn't have run with your interview. I should have asked you or I could have interviewed someone else. The editor asked me to apologize. She's really sorry you feel bad."

"She's sorry I feel bad or she's sorry for what she did?"

"The second one. She sees it was wrong. And we're all learning here, we're not professionals."

"What about you? How do you feel?"

"I told you I was sorry."

"No, you didn't."

"Okay, I thought I did. I'm sorry. I'm profusely sorry. I'm unbelievably filled with remorse. To the brim. Remorse is spilling over. How do I get you to believe me? Seriously, Treha, if I'd known how hurt you'd be, I would never have run it. I'm sorry."

Treha looked at the floor. "All right."

Anna handed her a printed page. "Look at this."

Treha glanced at it. "What is it?"

"Read it. They're all letters responding to your article. The praise is effusive. Like that word? They're talking about how real and honest you were. How it took courage to say what you said. This doesn't excuse my mistake — I'm not saying that — but people really liked it. Are they saying this to your face?"

"Some have said nice things," Treha said.

"Look at the last one. Down here at the bottom." Anna took the letter and held it up to the light and read. " 'Treha is one of the reasons I'm glad I chose this school. You can hear her heart coming through. Honored to be attending Bethesda with her.' "

"That's nice."

"No, look at who wrote it."

Treha stared at the name under the sentences. Cameron Goodman.

"That's right! Your heartthrob. He's practically asking you out in the school newspaper. You can read right between the lines."

Treha's face flushed and she took the page back to study the words.

"My editor said she wants to see anything you write," Anna said. "Even if it's a grocery list."

Treha was reading Cameron's words again. "You said you could introduce me to him."

"Well, I kind of stretched the truth."

"Anna."

"I'm sorry. I didn't mean to make you think I have this big relationship with him. But I'll see what I can do."

"No, don't. Let it happen naturally. That would be better."

"Are you sure? I can put a note on his lunch tray or something."

She shook her head. "Can I keep this?"

"The letters? Sure. And what do you think of writing for the paper? I could help you get started on something. We have a weekly column that any student can guest write, or you could do an opinion piece."

Treha stared at the page as she walked into the stairwell and didn't respond. She read Cameron's words again and sat with the paper in the courtyard with the wind swirling and the leaves in the trees swaying in the sunshine. The whole day somehow looked a little brighter.

Treha was in the cafeteria when it happened. With her back to the buffet line and a lunch of salad and yogurt. Someone passed her table — just a shadow at first, then she spotted Cameron, all dimples, white teeth, and those eyes. She had heard that the eyes were the windows to the soul but most people kept the shades drawn. Cameron didn't. He was an open book.

"Is this seat taken?"

She shook her head.

He reached out a hand. "I'm Cameron."

She shook his hand and looked at her salad.

"I saw the interview you gave in the *Tower.* Sounds like God is doing some good stuff in your life."

Treha stared at her fork, unable to speak.

"I can see it now," he said. "Your eyes. I see the movement. But it's not that bad. I wouldn't have noticed if you hadn't talked about it in the interview."

She looked up, just a little, and focused on his hair. Wavy, curly, with a mind of its own. Like he could get up in the morning and not even put a hand through it and it would look like that.

"It's better than it used to be. But it's not totally gone."

"Have you always had it?"

She nodded. "As long as I can remember."

"Do you know what caused it?"

"The doctors weren't sure. It might be my genes. Or it could have been the drugs my mother took before I was born."

She hadn't told anyone at school about this, and here she was giving away the most intimate information to someone she barely knew. But those dimples and that smile and those eyes dragged the truth from her.

He took a bite of pork barbecue and crunched his chips. So free. So effortless. Everything seemed to glide with Cameron — the way he walked, his speech, the way he ate. Treha looked at her food and suddenly worried that she would do something wrong, that she might find an awkward piece of lettuce.

"How did you discover that? I mean, if you don't know who your mother is, how could you know she took drugs?"

"She wrote me a letter and told me some things. And there was a doctor I knew, an old man I cared for, who was the one who gave my mother the drugs."

"This was in Arizona?"

"Yes."

"So you don't have any idea who your father is either, right?"

Treha nodded, then shook her head, confused as to how to communicate. "I don't know my father either. That's right."

"Do you want to know?"

"I suppose."

"Not knowing makes knowing your heavenly Father even more important, huh?"

"I'm learning more about that."

"Have you read Psalm 68?"

"I don't think so."

"This is really cool." He dug into his backpack and came up with a Bible that was falling apart. He flipped to the middle while he took another bite of barbecue, effortlessly turning the pages with a free hand. "I read a couple of psalms each day, and this was one from yesterday — no, two days ago."

He read the passage and his voice was like music, gentle and soft and inviting. " 'Father to the fatherless, defender of widows — this is God, whose dwelling is holy. God places the lonely in families; he sets the prisoners free and gives them joy.' Isn't that good?"

"Yes." Something inside Treha felt like it was coming to life. She took a bite of yogurt and finished her salad as they talked. Maybe it wasn't something coming alive as much as it was her getting used to the possibility that she could actually fit in here. Or maybe fit with someone like Cameron.

He glanced at his watch. "I have to get going. Maybe I'll see you around at the commons?"

"Okay," Treha said.

She watched him glide toward the rear of the cafeteria and put his dishes away and ease through the back door. And she couldn't suppress the warm feeling that spread through her and made her want to smile. She wanted to talk with someone about it, but Anna wasn't the person. She wanted to call Miriam or talk with Elsie, but would they understand?

Treha hadn't learned much about prayer before coming to Bethesda, but Elsie had modeled a simple, everyday conversation with God where you simply talked with him like a friend. Her professor for Spiritual Life and Disciplines, a required course for every incoming student, said writing out your prayers was a good way to discover what was really on your heart. So Treha dug out her spiral notebook and started to write.

God, I can't think of anything else but C. And this frustrates me because I know deep inside that it's probably just a dream, just an infatuation, and that he could never really like someone like me. I'm not pretty and I have a hard time talking to people and looking them in the eye. But I can't help thinking that these feelings are something you put inside. There's something good about them. But if I can't study because he's all I'm thinking about, that's not good. So would you help me focus on what's important and true?

The professor had given them a verse from Philippians to memorize. Treha didn't know it by heart yet but she carried it on a scrap of paper with her and pulled it out.

And now, dear brothers and sisters, one final thing. Fix your thoughts on what is true, and honorable, and right, and pure, and lovely, and admirable. Think about things that are excellent and worthy of praise.

Treha went back to her notebook and wrote, *I just realized that with C. overwhelming my thoughts, I haven't been thinking as much about my mother. Thank you, God, for letting me think of something else for a change.*

Chapter 12

Paige

Resolve is a terrible thing to waste, especially after talking to your mother. And so, throughout the restless nights leading up to my second class with Treha, I wrestled with the *how* of approaching her. Finally I opted to write a note on her essay, asking her to stay after class. My hands had trembled as I put the words down.

Treha was one of the last to arrive Monday night, and I worried that she wouldn't come. As I waited, glancing at the clock, still holding Treha's essay, I saw her picture on the front page of a student's copy of the *Tower.* It looked like a cross between a student photo and a mug shot. Beside it were the words "New Students Sound Off."

I considered asking to look at the article, wanting to read every word, in between the lines and in the margins. But right then Treha walked into the room and hurried behind me toward her seat. I held out her essay and said her name. She looked at me with a frightened deer look, took the paper, and headed to her seat.

Tonight's discussion was about conflict in stories, conflict in people's lives, and how that propels the writer and reader. The irony was not lost on me.

During my lecture I heard a phone beep, which irritated me. But when it beeped again, all I could do was sheepishly dig in my purse and say, "I'm not sure how to handle a professor who doesn't follow her own rules about cell phones."

The class laughed.

I turned the phone off and kept going. It was a good discussion, though I wished Treha would participate. I longed to engage with her, to hear her thoughts — about literature, about anything. She spent most of the class with her eyes on the desktop. I thought her posture looked like she was tuned into the discussion, but it was hard to tell.

At the end I gave their next assignment. They were to write an essay about a conflict in their own lives that had propelled them toward change. While others used their phones or computers to record the assignment, Treha wrote it in her notebook. She lingered at her desk as the other students headed for the door.

When we were the last two left, she pulled out the essay I had returned to her. "You wanted to see me?"

"Yes." I swallowed. "I wanted to tell you how much I liked your essay. And what you're bringing to this class. Would you like to take a seat?"

Treha gathered her things and moved to a desk in the front row. I pulled my desk chair up to sit in front of her.

"I can tell from what you've written that there's a lot to your story. I'm looking forward to reading the *Tower* article about you."

"I wish you wouldn't," Treha said.

"Why not?"

"Because I didn't want an article. I was told my picture wouldn't be there and my name wouldn't be used. I said things I wouldn't have."

"I don't think anyone will fault you for being honest."

"My roommate does."

"I see."

The silence between us deepened and I felt a tug on my soul, a frayed thread that begged to be pulled. "Sometimes opening up and revealing yourself is a good thing," I managed. "You could think of it that way."

She shrugged, picking at the strap on her backpack. "My friend wants me to write something for the paper."

I nodded. "I think you should. I've only read one essay, but in it you showed an ability to write lean and clean. That's not the norm. Most creative writing students are taught that good writing is effusive and . . ." I glanced at Treha.

"I know what it means."

"Right. Of course you do. In high school you're taught that the more adjectives and adverbs and descriptive words you use, the better. A wide vocabulary usually wins writing competitions. I have to retrain students to not write every big word they've learned. Less is more."

"Maybe it's a good thing I didn't go to high school."

I felt my eyes widen. "You didn't?"

"I went to elementary school when I was in the foster system, but when I reached middle school, I was moved around so much I didn't finish."

"Then how were you able to come here?"

"I learned how to read on my own, mostly, and once you learn to read, you can do anything."

I couldn't help but smile. "I agree. So you

got your GED?"

Treha nodded.

"That's wonderful. You've done so well, Treha. You're gifted; I hope you know that."

"I don't think of myself as gifted."

My eyes threatened to fill. I turned away for a moment, acting like I was picking at something in my eye. Then I said, "The best writing gets out of the way and lets the reader into the story. That's what pulls people in and makes them turn pages, makes them want to experience your life, your thoughts. That's what you did in this essay. May I see it again?"

Treha handed me the paper and I read her words about her mother, willing my voice not to shake. "I love this part. 'I wanted all my questions answered and everything wrapped and tied with a bow. But life is not neat bows and nice packages. Life is messy and you don't get all your questions answered.' " I gave the essay back. "That really sums up life in a way that most people your age don't get. How did you learn this?"

"I don't know." Treha put up a hand. "Wait, I said that to get more time to think."

I laughed. More than one student had already been challenged with my rule about those words. Apparently she had been pay-ing attention. "All right, go on."

"I learned from the people I've worked with. At the retirement home. I picked up a lot from one woman, Elsie, and from Miriam."

"And who is Miriam?"

"She's the one who gave me a job at Desert Gardens. She and Charlie let me stay at their home. Charlie is her husband."

"They sound like wonderful people."

Treha nodded. "I miss them. I miss talking with them. Learning from them. I have people who care. Maybe that's what you mean when you say I am gifted."

I reached out to take her hand but stopped myself at the last second. "Can you tell me about your mother? What do you know?"

"My adoption was private. She gave me away when I was a newborn. I don't know anything about her except for a letter she wrote. We've tried following the trail, different leads, but I don't think I'll ever know."

"Do you still have that letter?"

Treha unzipped her backpack and pulled out a worn envelope. "My friend Miriam kept the original, but I made this copy. I keep it with me."

I took the envelope, started to open it, then hesitated. "Do you mind?"

When Treha shook her head, I unfolded

the page inside, staring at the cursive writing.

My dearest Treha,

I don't know when you will read this letter. I don't know when your mother will give it to you, but I'm praying you will be ready to read it. I imagine your head is full of questions about yourself, about the family you've grown up in, and about me.

You are my heart. You are everything good in the world. And my heart breaks in writing this because I will not know you. Your first steps, your first words. I won't get to hold you or take pictures or see you off to school and cry over you. . . .

So many emotions returned as I read the letter. Hurt. Anger. It was a bottle I had thrown into the ocean of my life and never expected to have return, but here it was. I stared at the words, my own handwriting, and the feelings came back like an ocean wave. The depression. The medication I had taken. I had put my daughter at great risk, though the doctor assured me there was none. That letter was the only gift she had from me, other than her eye color and her love of reading.

I reached into my purse for a packet of tissues and held one to my nose.

"Allergies are terrible," Treha said.

I wanted to hug her. I wanted to envelop her. In my bursting heart was the inclination to cross the boundary between professor and mother, to let the curtain fall or rip from top to bottom. But I knew for Treha's sake I had to tread lightly.

I glanced at the pages again. "Have you always had this?"

"No, the woman who adopted me had it. I thought she was my real mother. But when I found out she had adopted me, I was glad. I don't want my mother to be like her."

Looking down at the wad of tissues in my lap, I said, "What do you want your mother to be like, Treha?"

Treha shrugged. "I don't . . . I guess I don't need her to be like anything. I want her to be herself."

"But if you could choose some qualities, if you could choose someone you know to be your mother, who comes close?"

She thought a moment. "My friend Miriam. She's like a mother. She helped me find a job and let me stay at her house when I was fired. I think that's what a mother is, someone who finds you. Who sees you. Even though I'm not everything a mother would want."

"What do you mean?"

"I'm not like everyone else. My roommate. The other students. The families I lived with. I've always known I make people uncomfortable. I wouldn't want to have a daughter like me."

"Treha, that's not . . ." I started to reach for her again but settled for clutching the tissues. "In your essay there was this longing to find her. Talk with her. I'm just wondering . . . If you could meet her, when you saw her, what would you say?"

Treha closed her eyes. "I wouldn't say anything."

"Really? I would think you'd have a thousand questions."

"Yes, I would. But if I found her, I don't think the questions would matter. It's like my theology professor says. We think we'll have questions for God when we get to heaven, but when we actually see him, we'll understand it's not about getting our questions answered because the questions won't be important. We'll finally be with God. So I would just look at her. And if she let me, I would hug her. For a long time."

I turned my head and pulled another tissue from the packet. When I thought I had myself under control, I looked at my daughter again. "Treha, I need to tell you something."

Her face wasn't angelic or cherubic. It was plain. It was pale and friendless, her eyes twitching slightly, searching.

The door opened at the front of the room and a hulk of a man entered. Darnelle Carter, the Bethesda security chief — a no-nonsense but gentle soul that everyone called D. C. Biceps like phone poles and the thighs of an NFL running back.

"Pardon me, Ms. Redwine." He spoke with a bit of a drawl and resonance like a bass drum. "We had a call for you at the office. An emergency."

His voice echoed through his chest and into the empty room.

"What emergency?"

"It's your mother, trying to get in touch. She said she couldn't reach you on your cell."

"My mother?" Right — my cell phone had beeped earlier in class. I fumbled in my purse and eventually found the phone and turned it on.

"It sounded important, ma'am, or I wouldn't have bothered you."

"No, that's all right. I'm glad you did. I just . . ."

There was a voice mail but my phone wouldn't retrieve it properly.

"The reception can be spotty in here, ma'am. Would you like to use the phone in our office?"

"Sure." I stood and gathered my things, wondering what might be awaiting me on the other end of the phone line. I turned to Treha. "I'm sorry."

"Go, call your mother," Treha said.

The words stung. I was calling my mother when Treha didn't have one or didn't know she was standing right in front of her.

D. C. opened the door again and let Treha go ahead of us.

With each footstep I felt like I was losing something, an opportunity perhaps. I nearly called out to her and asked her to wait. I could see it in my mind. Hugging her. Looking in her eyes. Saying, *Treha, I'm your mother. I'm so sorry it's taken me this long to reach out to you.* Something like that.

But I didn't. I let her go.

When we were outside, I tried my phone again but the reception still wasn't good. It wasn't until I reached the security office that I realized I had kept Treha's copy of my letter to her.

Chapter 13

Treha

After her talk with Ms. Redwine, Treha felt hungry and went to the commons but everything was closed. She didn't want to eat from a vending machine so she walked across campus to a gas station/convenience store. Students came here when they missed meals or needed snacks. She looked for fruit and a premixed salad.

She chose a large green apple after looking through the entire batch. The salad looked wilted and the stale date was today, but there wasn't a good alternative, so she went to the register at the front. Passing the candy aisle, she heard a familiar voice.

"Treha!"

Goose bumps rose on her flesh and she rubbed her arms but forgot she had an apple and a salad in her hands. "Hello, Cameron."

"You're hungry too, huh?" he said. "I

drew the short straw with the guys. We were watching the football game and needed some chips and something to drink." He looked at the salad and apple. "You don't need much, do you?"

"No, just something to make me not hungry so I can sleep."

He got out his wallet. "Here, let me pay for that."

She started to say no, but he took the salad and apple and put them on the counter before she could.

"Anything else for you two?" the cashier said, looking at both of them as if they were a couple, and Treha thought it was a most wonderful feeling to be seen with someone like Cameron and be mistaken for his girlfriend.

The cashier put their things in bags and Cameron swiped his card. In the parking lot he rearranged things, putting Treha's apple and salad in a separate bag. They walked back to campus together, and Cameron chatted about his classes, the discussions and reading he'd found most challenging. Treha tried to think of something to say, some way to respond that would show how interested she was in him, that would invite him into her life. But all she could do was nod.

"I must sound pretty boring."

"I like to hear you talk."

He smiled. They were on the quad now, standing in front of the tower under the oak tree that spread out like a canopy. Light from the tower and well-placed lamps illumined the quad in a soft glow, and the moon was full and gave its own luster to the surroundings. The days were getting shorter as they moved toward fall and winter.

Cameron turned and looked at her. "There's something I've been meaning to ask you."

Treha felt her heart flutter. The voice, the smile, the dimples, the hair. In a flash she could see herself with him. She really could. And it wasn't something she had manufactured. She'd just run into him at the convenience store. He had noticed her. It was all here, something that could never happen but was happening. A fairy tale come true. She wanted to call Miriam right then.

"I'm a little nervous to bring this up," he said, "because I don't know how you'll respond."

She searched his eyes. She could see them with children who were not like her but normal and happy. People would marvel that a guy like him, who could have any girl, would choose her.

"Go ahead," Treha said. "You don't have to be afraid."

He switched the bags with soda to the other hand and flexed his fingers. "Okay, I'll just come out with it. You're roommates with Shelly, right?"

Treha stared.

"I had one class with her last year and I could never get up the nerve to even talk to her. But I can tell she's really amazing and I'd like to get to know her better."

"That's what you wanted to ask me?"

"Well, I wanted to see if you would put in a good word for me. Like, maybe suggest that it would be a good thing if we would go out or something."

Treha looked up at the tower. She could see it through the trees, the light leaking through and casting a romantic glow.

Cameron put down the bag with the soda in it and reached into his pocket. "And I have this." He pulled out an envelope. "But I don't want to give it to her until it's the right time, you know? Until I know she might be interested."

"What does it say?"

"It's just a card with some things I've noticed about her. I mean, I don't want to scare her and make her think I'm stalking her. But I can't get her out of my mind. I think maybe God wants us together. I had a dream one night . . . Now that will really freak her out — a guy dreaming about her. I don't want to come on too strong. Do you think you could, I don't know, maybe talk with her?"

Treha held out a hand. "Let me have it."

Cameron handed the card to her and smiled. "Thank you. You don't know what this means." He reached out and drew her in, hugging her. "You're so easy to talk with, Treha. I wish talking with Shelly were this easy."

She smelled the musky cologne he wore and his hair brushed her face. She didn't look up or return the hug, but he didn't notice.

"Don't give her this unless you're sure she's interested. You know, talk to her . . . Of course you will. I trust you."

She slipped the card into the bag with the dinner he had paid for.

"Thank you so much," he said.

Treha watched him run to his dorm, plastic grocery bags flapping as he leaped up the steps and bolted into the building. She turned and went into the commons but her regular booth was occupied. People in every area and she wanted to be alone. She went back to the dorm and found her room empty.

She dug the envelope out of the bag. On the front he'd written *Shelly.* She never would've imagined how one word could cut so deeply. His handwriting wasn't that good. Just scrawl, really. She sniffed the card and smelled his cologne. Then she closed her eyes and felt his embrace. If only this card had been written to her. If only he had hugged her because he was interested in her. But who was she kidding. Why would any guy be interested in her?

The flap was sealed. She got her finger underneath and tried to pry it open, but it tore at the top and she was so angry that she ripped the whole thing. Then she regretted it and wondered how she could ever explain.

She pulled out the card. It was printed on recycled cardboard, eco-friendly. That's what it said on the back. There was a little heart on the front, raised off the surface. Just two red lines that didn't connect.

The inside had no words printed but plenty scrawled. The sentences began on the left side and went all the way to the right in an upward slant and started over again.

Shelly,

I remember the first time I saw you. I remember the feeling deep inside of seeing the most beautiful girl in the world. All I could do was stare. At your hair and how silky smooth it was.

Treha felt sick. Cameron actually wrote about Shelly's hair? He should try to live with the smell of the shampoo she used wafting through their dorm.

I've tried to get up the nerve to talk with you, other than just saying hello, but I can't. Each time you asked a question or spoke to your friends, each time I heard your voice, it was like Elizabeth when Mary came to her house — something inside leaped within me.

Treha rolled her eyes. She couldn't read the rest. It was like all the bad, sentimental writing of romance novels. Glancing at the bottom, she noticed he hadn't signed it. Just drew a smiley face that kind of looked like the heart-swish on the front. She closed the card and looked at the bag with the food Cameron bought for her. She couldn't eat it. Not after seeing his shallow heart.

She tossed the card into the wastebasket by her desk, then took the bag with the food in it and dropped it down the trash chute in the hall. She heard Shelly's voice and quickly returned to her room, crawling into bed without changing and feeling like her life was over.

Chapter 14

Paige

D. C. handed me the phone and left me alone in the security office. I took a deep breath as I dialed.

"Yes — hello?"

A mother's voice is supposed to soothe and calm. A mother's voice is supposed to convey love at the deepest level of our existence. But a mother's voice can also feel like fingernails on the soul's blackboard.

"Mom, it's me. What's wrong?"

Her voice shook. "I tried to call your cell phone. I left a message. And when I didn't hear back, I got worried. I didn't mean to alarm you."

"It's okay. What's wrong? Has something happened to Dad?"

"Yes — oh, Paige, I don't want to burden you with any more than you already have. . . ."

"What happened?"

"Something's not right. He's been agitated. I thought it was a reaction to his medication or something he ate. But he took a turn and became aggressive."

"That's not like him."

"Of course it's not. He's the gentlest soul ever."

"Did he hurt you?"

"No, he would never do that."

"Mom, be honest. This is the disease, not him. Did he hurt you?"

"He left the house, Paige."

"Left? I thought he couldn't walk."

"Yes — well, evidently he can, and when I caught up to him outside, he pushed me. I don't think he knew what he was doing."

"Did you fall?"

"It's nothing. Just a scrape on my arm."

"Mom."

More emotion in her voice. "I'm scared. About what might happen. What's going to happen."

"Mom, this was inevitable. I told you things would get worse."

"Don't tell me 'I told you so.' You're not living this. I am."

I closed my eyes. "Where is he now?"

"I called the police and they found him wandering around. He only had his bathrobe and his boxers on. His slippers. He's not in his right mind, Paige."

She broke down and her sobs reached an empty place in my heart. I wanted to be angry at her. I wanted this to be some imagined crisis she was making up. I wanted to reassure her that everything would be all right. But I couldn't.

"I'm coming down there."

"No, I don't want you to worry. I know you have your teaching, your classes, the dissertation. I have friends at church who are helping. We're going to be fine."

"I need to be there."

"Paige, that's not why I called."

"I don't care why you called. I want to be there."

I said it more forcefully than I intended, but sometimes Mom will only listen to a raised voice.

"Where is he now?" I said.

"The hospital. They're still observing him." She went into what the doctors had said, the possible reasons why he had wandered away, and then moved on to what floor he was on and the minutiae of medication changes and procedures and things I didn't need to know, but I let her talk and the more she did, the more calm she grew, more sane. When she came up for air, she said something that shocked me.

"Have you talked to her?"

"Have I talked to whom?"

"The girl. Your daughter." She nearly choked on the word.

"When I got your message, I was in the middle of a conversation."

"So she knows?"

"Not yet. I want to be sensitive to her and not just blurt things out."

"I think that's wise. You need to give it time. Choose the right moment."

I had been waiting a couple decades for the right moment. I had waited more than a year from the time I discovered where she lived to make contact, and even then it wasn't from my volition. Would there ever be a "right moment"?

I steered the conversation back to my father, but she wouldn't let go. "I need to know you're not going to tell her. Just for now, until we get through this crisis with your father."

"You don't know what you're asking."

"Yes, I do. I know you want to get this off your chest and I can understand that. I really can. I've been thinking about it and I don't want to hold you back from what you need to do. But can you wait until we get through this?"

"Did you talk with Dad about it?"

"Paige, he doesn't understand. You haven't seen him like this. I'm not accusing — this is just reality. I talk with him. I have this running conversation about his medication and appointments and what he wants to eat. I don't have anyone else, so I talk to him, but he doesn't take it in. He's like a rock. My words bounce off."

"But you told him I found his granddaughter."

"Of course. Who else am I supposed to talk to? I can't share this with anyone except him and God."

"And what does God say, Mom? What does he think about this?"

"How can you be so cruel? I'm at my most vulnerable. My lowest point. And you want to kick me."

"I didn't mean it that way." I took another breath and put a hand to my head. "I'm sorry. I didn't mean to upset you. I love you. I want to be there for you. I'm hopping on the next plane."

"No, don't do that. You have your classes."

"Someone else can take my classes. I'll call the department head and explain. It's a family emergency."

"You have your writing. I know that's taking up a lot of your time."

Not enough of it, I thought. "There are

more important things than my dissertation. You're one of them. If I can be there to help —"

"It's going to be too expensive to fly on short notice."

That was all I needed. "When is he being released?"

"Wednesday, perhaps. That's what the doctor said. Best-case scenario. But they want me to install some locks and have some safety precautions so he can't do this again. They're talking about a home health nurse to monitor him. I don't know how much that's going to cost."

"I'll make the reservation and be there tomorrow. I'll help you sort out the insurance and everything."

"Yes — but I don't think it's necessary."

"I'm coming, Mom."

"Well, if you insist. Just let me know when your flight arrives and I'll —"

"I'll rent a car and come to you. You won't have to do a thing."

"Now that's an added expense you don't need."

"Don't worry, Mom. I'm a big girl. We'll figure this out together, okay?"

"Yes — well, all right."

I thought that was the end. I thought the possibility of my presence would soothe her, but she returned to the original request.

"Will you promise me you won't talk with her before you come? Can you promise that?"

I hadn't done well with promises. I had promised that I would guard my purity when I was younger. I'd worn the ring my father had given me. But that ring was off and buried somewhere in a keepsake box in their condo's attic. I had promised myself and God that if he ever gave me the chance to meet my daughter, I would take it. And that hadn't worked out too well.

"All right, Mom, you win. I won't talk with her before I leave."

"You don't know how much that comforts me, Paige. Thank you for doing this."

I hung up and found D. C. outside the office and thanked him.

"Is everything all right, ma'am?"

"It's my father. I need to head down there for a few days. I think he'll be okay, though."

"I'm glad you're doing that, ma'am. That sounds like a good plan."

Maybe it was. Maybe it wasn't. Maybe I was saying yes because I wanted to reach out to my parents. Maybe I had said yes because I wanted to run away.

Chapter 15

Treha

Treha awoke to rain and a crack of thunder in the distance. The sound made her want to stay in bed and hide from the world. It made her want to stay in bed the rest of her life. The pitter-pat of water against the window brought a certain comfort, a repetitive *tick-tick-tick* that soothed her brain. She envied others who could awaken, yawn, then roll over and go back to sleep. She'd never been able to do that.

There was a chill in the air, an early portent of the approaching winter. But there was something cold in her soul that had nothing to do with the rain or falling temperatures. It was warm beneath the covers, so she stayed there a few moments, thinking about what had happened the night before.

She hadn't laid out her clothes, and she'd slept in what she'd worn all day Monday. She needed a shower. Her hair was tousled.

Forget her hair. Forget brushing her teeth. What was the point? She just had to start moving before Shelly did.

The thin carpet was cold when her feet hit the floor and she stood there, a strange feeling in the pit of her stomach. She was angry with Shelly for the way she treated her. She was angry that Shelly could draw guys like honey draws ants. But that wasn't the real problem. What angered her most was that Cameron could be interested in Shelly, would think that she was a good fit.

Treha went to the trash where she had tossed the card but it wasn't there. She stared at the trash can. Had she tossed it down the chute? She was sure she had thrown it here by her desk. Her heart fluttered when she thought of it mixed in with the other trash in the basement bins and what it would take to find it.

She had to let it go, just move on without letting it consume her. Everyone made mistakes. Her heart was broken. Cameron would understand.

As she moved toward the commons, doubt crept in. Would she have the nerve to tell him what she had done? She sat in her regular booth and pulled out her journal. The thoughts spinning in her head would make a good column, if she decided to write for the paper. "When Others Let You Down" could be the title, with the point being that everyone was fallible. Everyone made mistakes. Trust God, not people. But that sounded harsh and was probably not best for public consumption.

She started writing anyway, just for herself, and was so focused that she didn't see who approached and sat across from her.

"Hi," Cameron said. "You're up early."

His voice startled her. "I'm always up at this time."

"That's a good habit. Some people pull all-nighters, but I have to wonder if they're really getting anything done or if they'll retain any of that information."

Treha nodded. When she didn't speak, Cameron shifted in his seat.

"How did you like the salad?"

Treha shrugged.

"Yeah, I've had some of their food before and it wasn't the greatest. . . ." He hesitated, then said, "So . . . I was wondering if you had a chance to talk with Shelly."

He looked like a nervous cat. And then she noticed the dimples. The smile. Hair with a mind of its own, but what a wonderful mind. One look was all it took to draw her back into the illusion. He was so easy to look at. And Treha knew she had a choice.

She could tell him what she had done or give him only a shade of the truth. She was ready to give him the whole truth but when she looked in his eyes, her resolve crumbled.

"I didn't see her last night," she said. "I went to sleep as soon as my head hit the pillow."

"What a relief!" Cameron wiped his face with his hands and sighed, slumping down into the booth. He laughed. He actually laughed through his hands. "You won't believe this. I was up all night worried about it. What she'd say. How she'd react. The fact that I didn't sign the thing. I put this goofy drawing at the bottom. It was infantile, the whole thing. Asking you to talk with her was a weak thing to do. So don't say anything. I shouldn't have asked you to do that."

"It's okay. I didn't talk with her."

"Great. I can sleep again. I just need the card back. Do you have it with you?"

"No . . . I must have left it in the room."

"Okay. Could you get it? I know it's a lot to ask. I just need to have it."

The rain was coming down sideways outside. "I usually don't go back to the room before class. I don't like to disturb her."

"But can you just slip in? It would mean a lot."

"I can't. But I promise she won't see it."

There was pain on his face now. "Girls want a man, not a boy. And I was acting like a scared kid. The more I thought about it, the more I want to wait. Do this my own way. You know, be strong."

"Well, it's probably better that you talk with her. We don't have the best relationship. She doesn't want to be my roommate."

"Why not? I would think you'd be the perfect roommate."

The words warmed her. Funny how something said so innocently could feel like a microwave inside. "I'm not the perfect anything."

"Treha, you're amazing. You're one of the coolest people on campus. If she doesn't think you're a good roommate, there must be something wrong with her."

Now he was on the right track. Now he was getting it. Shelly wasn't the right person for him.

"So when can you get the card back to me?"

She looked at her notebook as if her schedule were there. "Later. Maybe after dinner? It's a busy day."

"Okay." He wrote something on a piece of paper. "Here's my phone number. Call or text me as soon as you have it, okay?"

Treha nodded.

Before he left, he turned and said, "I really appreciate you not saying anything. You're a good friend, Treha."

She tried to smile, but smiling wasn't easy. When he left, Treha headed for the dorm trash bins.

CHAPTER 16

Paige

The plane was full and I sat beside a mother with her two-year-old, who clearly didn't understand the concept of personal space. I was hoping for some time to think and prepare myself for what was ahead, but instead I encountered screaming and tantrum throwing and cereal tossing and ugly stares from people around us who evidently thought I was part of the problem. Missing this part of motherhood was not a bad thing.

Dr. Waldron had been understanding when I informed him of my sudden departure. He said the right words and even conveyed the compassion due the situation, and yet I sensed unease.

"Let me get on the ground and find out where this is going," I'd said. "I'll know more when I get there."

"Yes. I know you need to do this, Paige, and I'm glad you're going. I really am."

But. Such a small word that hangs in the air of most conversations. *But* our agreement stands. *But* you need to finish the writing. *But* your employment is on the line.

I heard the *but* resounding in my head as I stared out the window and remembered the long, tortuous trip from New Guinea. I had taken a series of unending flights, my stomach bulging and everything falling apart around me. There'd been stares on those flights as well. People looking at my age, my youth, and my pregnancy. I'd wanted to crawl into an overhead bin.

When I pulled up in my rental car, my mother met me at the door of their condo and gave me a tepid hug and a side kiss. I could tell some of the weight had lifted from her as I walked inside, but the past few days had taken their toll. No, the past few years.

"Any news?" I said.

"They're saying tomorrow morning. They think he's stabilized."

"That's good."

"The man from the security company is coming — should be here within the hour. They've had a lot of experience with this kind of thing — that's what they told me — so I'm hoping they can help us keep him corralled. I'm not sure of the cost, though."

"Mom, we'll do what we need to do."

"Yes — I'm nervous about punching all the numbers. I've seen these things in a friend's house and there's so much to remember. If you don't do it correctly, the alarm rings and they send out guards."

My mother had skinned wild hogs and cooked them over a spit. She'd killed snakes that weighed more than she did. But until recently she hadn't been able to pump her own gasoline. She didn't know how to swipe her credit card and punch in the zip code. The world had gotten more complicated and left her sitting in the slow lane wondering where the next rest area might be.

"I can help you with that, Mom. Don't worry. They'll make it as easy as they can. We'll write everything down."

We talked about Dad's condition and I asked to see the scrape on her arm. She protested, said it was nothing, said it was hard to see it in a long-sleeved shirt. Finally she relented, and the bruise took my breath away. It extended from her wrist to her elbow and had turned a deep purple.

"You look like you went a couple of rounds with Mike Tyson. This is awful."

"It's nothing, really," she said.

"Did you have that looked at? It could be broken."

"I'd be in more pain if it were broken. I

was a nurse, you know."

She had worked as a nurse in the jungle, though she'd had scant training before leaving the States. She did know injuries when she saw them. Bones protruding. Inadvertent machete gashes. She'd even done an amputation, though the patient hadn't lived long afterward. I insisted she go to urgent care, but she wasn't having it.

Finally she said, "Paige, we need to stop bickering and pull together. Our mission is to get your father home and get him settled. Let's put our differences aside. And don't try to boss me like I'm a child."

"I'm just concerned. For both of you."

"Well, we've been doing all right without you for quite a while."

So much for pulling together, I thought. If my father was a connoisseur of words, my mother was an aficionado of guilt. She baked with it, stirring and folding it into every relationship, and to be honest, it was working.

"Now, while I wait here for the security company, you go up to your father's study and get some work done. We fixed him a nice room up there before he got sick."

"You make it sound like I've never seen it before."

"Of course you have, but I'm just saying

— have a look. It's a shame he can't go there. I keep a gate here in the closet, the kind to block little children. It's been more than a year since he's been up there."

"You shouldn't be living in a two-story."

She gave me a look and I put both hands in the air. "Sorry. One for all and all for one."

"It's nice and peaceful there. When he takes a nap, I go up and look over some old manuscripts and wood-working projects. It brings back good memories."

"I don't think I can work on my dissertation right now, Mom."

"Yes — well, if you can't work, go up there and rest. You remember the hammock he made — we hung it in the corner."

"The one we put between the hoop pines? How in the world did you get it?"

"It's a long story — a villager found it and gave it to a family returning for furlough. Your father used to sleep in that hammock. His favorite spot. Go on, you have to have a look."

I climbed the stairs and quickly ducked into their old bedroom, the one they'd had to abandon after the disease set in. It's hard watching your parents age. As a child I felt they would always stay the same, just like they thought about me. They'd been so vibrant, so full of life and questions. Now there were handrails along bathroom walls and telltale sights and smells of aging. The bedroom downstairs was used for easier access, but there were still signs of them in here. My mother's shoe collection. My father's shirts and pants that weren't worn any longer in baskets on the closet floor.

Down the hall was the extra bedroom they had turned into a study, and walking inside felt like going back in time. Pictures of people and scenes from our lives covered the walls. I closed my eyes and they came to life. The sounds of voices and insects and rain and wind and kumul birds in the trees. The feel of the earth under my bare feet.

On Dad's desk were his carving tools and several ink pens and raw pieces of wood, like someone had interrupted him in the middle of a project. Dementia is like Vesuvius. It strikes in the middle of whatever you're doing.

Next to his woodworking tools were the manuscripts, and beside them was a copy of the Bible, translated into the Sio language. I picked it up and flipped through the pages. Rarely can a person hold the words of one father, let alone two.

Finally I turned to the corner. Attached to two walls by metal hooks was the hammock, made from military green fabric, something my father had fashioned from leftovers of a forgotten war. I knelt on the floor and smelled the musty, musky fragrance still trapped in the cotton fibers. Immediately I was at the beach, in that hammock with *him.* Not my father. Treha's father. It was one of the places we'd gone on moonlit nights with the surf pounding the coral reef. I had seen my daughter the day before and now I was seeing the place where she had been conceived. Or at least one of the possible places. It could have been on the beach. It could have been in the L-shaped tree we climbed. In my room when my parents were away one morning. Good Christian girls are not supposed to do that. Especially missionary daughters. And if it happens, it's only supposed to happen once. And you're not supposed to enjoy it. You're supposed to come under such conviction that you stop. But we didn't.

"I think this is what I miss most," my mother said behind me. Her voice startled me and guilt rose that wasn't from her for once. She put a hand on my shoulder, her eyes on the desk. "Just seeing him sit there and work. He was always busy. His mind was always going, always trying to figure something out."

I moved away from the hammock and picked up one of the photo albums stacked beside the desk. Old photos of my parents. My mother's gap-toothed smile. She and my father on a date. My skinny, lanky dad down on one knee. A blurry photo of the two of them offering each other wedding cake. Then language school and a period of empty years skipped over before they finally had pictures of my mother pregnant, then me on a blanket, pudgy and drooling.

"I remember this airstrip," I said, pointing to a photo. "I remember the sound of the plane getting close and how we'd run out and wave. I remember you humming hymns and me trying to come up with the words."

"So you do have some good memories?"

I let the jab go. "If I close my eyes, I can see him at his workbench. It was the only thing he ever really did for himself, wasn't it?"

"Even that work wasn't for him. He made things for others. It's what made him happiest. If he wasn't translating or editing, he was fixing someone's roof." She picked up a block of wood. "But the pens were his favorite."

"I still have mine." I pulled it from my pocket and showed her. "My name is almost rubbed out, but you can still see the *P* and the *g.*"

She took it from me and smiled. "You sat with him and watched by candlelight. He would tell me how he loved watching you as your eyes got heavy and then he would carry you to bed and read you a story as you drifted off."

I stared at the pen, almost too afraid to say what I was thinking. "Deep in the night, I can still hear his voice. Echoes of his whispered prayers over me."

"Thank you, loving Father, for our Paige. Write your Word on her heart. You say in your Word that you store up success for the upright. Pour out your love on her and through her."

Mom skirted what I'd said. "He always said these pens were gifts that returned to the giver. He'd send them to supporters with a note." She said it sadly as if I didn't use the pen enough, as if I had forever missed a chance with my father. "The thing he never got to do was make toys for the grandkids. Blocks. A train. He talked about it. What it would be like to have children here. I guess that's never going to happen."

"You mean because of his condition or because I'm not having children?"

"I'm not blaming you. This is no one's fault. It's just . . . I guess it's God's will we're dealing with, isn't it?"

God's will. There was a topic of discussion that would probably tear us apart. "Dad always said it was the safest place you could be, didn't he?"

She nodded, looking at their wedding photo on the desk, her weathered fingers tracing the outline of his face through the gathered dust. "There was a witch doctor who tried to cast a spell on us. Did you know that?"

"I vaguely recall something about it."

"Your father told that story when we were on furlough, speaking at churches. He said he felt he was safer in some ways than those in quiet, suburban homes with picket fences. Our whole family was safer in the middle of God's will than anywhere else on the planet."

"How did you know it was God's will, Mom? To leave? To marry Dad?"

"I don't think it's some mysterious thing. It's not like he's trying to hide it. God presents his will in unlikely ways. Unlikely opportunities we have to obey or not. So it's my job to not get discouraged about the small thing I must do today. My job is to trust."

"What if you can't? In the middle of your husband wandering off or pushing you?"

"Some women have husbands who walk

away and exchange them for a newer model. My husband is drifting away a little at a time, and it's nothing he's chosen. He's fighting. He doesn't want to go. I think that's why he gets angry. But I don't know how it all works together, Paige. I've given up trying to understand the whys. You, for example. Why God let that happen. Why you had to go through so much pain."

"I made a mistake. Disobedience has consequences." I sighed. "Maybe we shouldn't have tried to hide it. Maybe I should have kept my daughter."

She put the picture down. "We did the best we could."

I stood with the silence between us, willing the words to come. "You would be proud of her, Mom."

"Let's not talk about this right now," she said.

I reached out for her arm, forgetting it was the bruised one. She recoiled in pain and I apologized. "We've never really talked about this. I think it would help me."

"Help you? How could it possibly make any difference after all these years?" She looked out the window, still holding the pen. "If you tell her who you are, you have to tell her about her father. You have to explain what happened. Which will lead to more questions."

"It will lead her to the truth."

"What truth?

"About herself. About how she came into the world."

"It will destroy his parents and what they thought, what they believed about his memory."

"Mom, they have a granddaughter they don't even know."

"You have no right to tarnish those people's lives. He got what he wanted. He didn't come back for you."

"He wrote me."

"Paige, let it go. There is nothing but pain ahead if you keep following this trail. For you. For all of us."

I looked out the same window and unexpected tears came to my eyes. "I was on the plane today and thought about myself as a scared seventeen-year-old. I see students at school in the throes of some first love experience or watch a film with some young actress the same age I was, and this sadness and loss comes over me. About who I was. How alone I was. And we could never talk."

"What's to talk about?"

I opened my mouth, searching for words, but they wouldn't come and I regretted bringing the whole thing up at such a time.

The doorbell rang. She looked at the floor, concentrating on each step as she moved to talk with the man installing the security system. He listened to her tell the story of my father, where he was, what medication he was on, his doctor's name, all the tiny aspects of his life she held in her mind because my father couldn't.

"Mom, he just needs to know where to put the alarm."

"Oh, I don't mind," the man said, but he was clearly grateful I had intervened.

I stayed with them as he explained the unit, what it was designed to do and what she would hear if the door was opened. "You'll hear this if he tries to go outside. That'll give you a warning and you can be ready."

I finally left them alone and wandered upstairs again, a thousand thoughts coursing through my mind. Surrounded by the faces of the past, I crawled into the hammock and went to sleep.

CHAPTER 17

Treha

Treha searched the trash bins as well as she could but had to hurry to class. Before dinner she put on her janitorial uniform, even though she wasn't on duty, and went to the Dumpsters outside her dorm, pawing through the bags. She didn't have gloves, so she used plastic shopping bags to keep from getting her hands wet.

She could have sworn she put the card in the trash by her desk. . . .

Why had she thrown it away? If only she hadn't. She should have seen the truth about Cameron and simply let him go.

She sat on the heap, thinking that this was where desire led. You want a boyfriend, you wind up getting your heart ripped open *and* you have to look through other people's trash.

Her heart fluttered when she saw a white bag with the familiar logo of the convenience store. Inside were the salad and apple. The receipt was also there, but no card.

On the way back inside, she met Anna coming from the library.

"Just the person I wanted to see," Anna said. "Didn't you get my messages? Have you been avoiding me?"

"I've been busy."

Anna frowned. "Too busy to write a column? My editor is still asking about you, Treha."

"I don't have anything to write about."

"I doubt that's true. There's probably something rolling around that brain. Some observation from the Treha treasure trove."

"It's more like Treha's trash."

"What do you mean?"

"Nothing." But the words gave her an idea. "When do you need it?"

"Tomorrow. Today would be better." Anna followed her. "So how's your love life?"

"What do you mean?"

"Somebody said you and Cameron were at the convenience store and he bought your dinner. Then I heard you two were sitting in the commons early this morning. I'd say that's the start of a beautiful relationship."

Treha stared at her. "How do you know all this?"

"That's part of being a reporter. You develop good sources that will tell you everything you need to know. So what's going on? Has he kissed you? Have you exchanged life verses? That's almost better than an engagement ring around here."

Treha took a deep breath. "He's not interested in me. He's interested in someone else."

"He told you that?"

Treha nodded.

"Then why would he spend time with you?"

"I need to clean up and work on the column. Okay?"

"Wait —"

"I don't want to become one of your sources."

Anna looked hurt. "I wouldn't share this with anybody. You can trust me."

"I need to go."

"All right, but if you want to talk about the Cameron thing, I'm here."

Treha didn't answer, but she heard real compassion in Anna's voice. She went back to her room. Shelly was there with a friend and they both stopped talking when she entered, so Treha grabbed her clothes and cleaned up in the bathroom, then moved to the lounge and sat on a love seat and pulled out her spiral notebook. Ms. Redwine said writing could help you process your life, but Treha wondered if that worked with the TV blaring and girls playing Taboo, laughing and giggling.

As soon as she put her pen to the page, something happened. Ideas and thoughts and words spilled like someone was pushing them out of her.

Last year I was working at a retirement home when the director got a frantic call from a man we both knew, one of the few people at the home who still had their driving privileges. He was stranded in a parking lot with temperatures nearing 100 degrees, a dangerous place for anyone, but especially the elderly. He couldn't find his car keys.

My friend told him to get to a cool place and wait. She and I drove to the parking lot and found him at a grocery store. The keys were not in his car — he had locked it, so he knew he had them with him when he left. He had eaten a sub sandwich, then visited a bookstore and finally bought groceries.

We asked at all three stores but no one had turned in the missing keys. We walked the sidewalk, went up and down all the aisles in the bookstore and grocery store, looked underneath the car and around it. The longer we looked, the more clear it became that our last option was the worst one. I went back to the restaurant and pulled the plastic trash bag out of the container near the front of the store. We took the bag to the Dumpster and lifted out each wrapper and uneaten piece of sandwich one by one. The old man protested and said he would never have thrown his keys away. It was silly for us to look here, he said, but I kept going, kept looking through the napkins and half-filled soda cups and leftovers. Bread and peppers and onions and tomatoes.

The longer I worked, the hotter it became. I wanted to give up, but something inside said not to. You should have seen his face when I shook out a yellow wrapper and his keys dropped to the pavement. It was one of the best sounds I've ever heard. He looked at me with gratitude, but the worry on his face overwhelmed us all.

Going through that trash wasn't easy, but I learned a lot that day.

Sometimes you have to deal with other people's trash. Sometimes, in order to love them, you have to dig through the unpleasant stuff and sort out the good from the bad. You have to get dirty.

Treha looked up and saw the resident adviser standing behind her, looking at what she was writing. Jill had been kind to her from the first day but hadn't spoken that much afterward.

"Treha, would you mind coming with me?"

"Why?"

"You'll see."

Treha closed the notebook and followed Jill. The RA's room was bigger and Treha wished she could have a place to herself like this. She was startled to see Shelly in the room. The look on her face was not kind, but when was it ever?

"Did I do something wrong?" Treha said.

"Why don't you have a seat?" Jill said.

Treha looked at Shelly. "I'll stand."

"Treha, we've found something disturbing. I'm hoping you could help us understand."

Shelly held out the card and ripped envelope. "You either opened my mail or it's worse than that."

Treha took the card from her, trying to think what "worse than that" could mean.

"Did you open this?" Jill said. "Did you

open Shelly's mail?"

Treha nodded.

"She admitted it," Shelly said. "Case closed."

"Did you have anything to do with writing it?" Jill said.

"No."

"Why did you open it?"

"I have a friend . . . he asked me to give this to Shelly. He has a crush on her."

"Who?" Shelly said.

Treha ignored the girl and kept looking at Jill.

"Shelly, let me have a few minutes alone with Treha."

"I can't believe this," Shelly said. "She's caught red-handed and you don't do a thing."

"Shelly, please."

Shelly got up and stomped out of the room and slammed the door.

"Okay, now will you sit?"

Treha nodded and took the seat Shelly had vacated.

"Tell me what happened."

Without revealing the writer of the card, Treha told Jill the story. How she had a crush on this particular guy and the guy wanted her to reach out to Shelly. "I was so angry with him, I threw it away instead of giving it to her. But I changed my mind and came back for it. But it was gone."

"Does he know you threw it away?"

"I talked with him this morning. He asked me to return the card because he'd changed his mind about reaching out to Shelly."

"Smart guy," Jill said.

Treha looked up and saw Jill's grin.

"What was she doing going through my trash can?" Treha said.

"You have a point. But Shelly said she saw her name on the envelope as she passed your desk. She said she wasn't snooping."

"And you believe her?"

"I don't think it matters. I was trying to keep you two together because, in some weird way, I thought you'd be a good influence on her. Maybe I should have separated you from the start."

"I'm okay with getting a new roommate."

Jill nodded. "The problem is, she's already taken this above me. They're going to want answers."

"For an envelope and card? He's said he doesn't want her to see it."

"But she has. And taking other people's personal property is a serious deal; you know that."

Treha looked at the floor.

"It would help to have the guy who wrote

the card come forward. Does he know you opened it and read it?"

"No."

"Okay. Do you think you can convince him to tell us the truth and clear this up?"

"I promised I wouldn't tell anyone who he is."

Jill bit the inside of her cheek. "Why don't you try, Treha? I'll try to keep the Shelly train in the station. But we need him to confirm your story."

CHAPTER 18

Paige

We brought my father home Wednesday afternoon. We got him into a wheelchair and his head bobbed and weaved like a prize-fighter as I pushed him up the incline from the garage into the house. When he was inside the kitchen, I hugged him and whispered in his ear, "We're so glad you're home, Dad."

I pulled back and looked him in the eyes but he wasn't there. My mother helped him into his favorite chair and we went on with life, the food, the news cycle, the daily duties. Mom began telling stories of his behavior in the past months that she couldn't on the first night. "If we lived in some colder climate, we wouldn't have him anymore, Paige. He woke me up a few weeks ago and said, 'So this is where you are!' It was three in the morning. And his feet were all muddy from walking around outside in the sprinkler trying to find me."

"We should have gotten you help then," I said.

"That's easy to say looking back, but I thought he was going through a phase. I started locking the front door and sleeping on the couch in the living room, hoping to head him off at the pass. Everything was fine for a while, and then early one morning I heard a crash. Scared me half to death. I thought we were being robbed. I walked into the pantry and found him on the floor with all sorts of ketchup and syrup and pickle bottles broken around him. I asked what he was doing in there and he said he was looking for the Christmas present he had hidden for you. Paige, he thought he was back in the jungle and that you were a little girl."

"What did you do?"

"I called the neighbors for help. I didn't know what to do. They rushed over here and found him sitting at the table. It was three thirty at that point. They helped calm him down and cleaned up the pantry. When they saw everything was under control, they got ready to leave. He calls out, 'Why are you taking off so early?' We were all exhausted. He was ready for me to make lunch."

I couldn't help smiling, thinking of him bewildered that anyone would be leaving the house.

"Now I'm waiting for the next episode. I don't want to keep him drugged so heavily he's a zombie, but I need to sleep."

I kept watch over him that first night and let her rest. After he had taken his medication and was ready for sleep, I sat beside him, held his hand, and read to him from the Bible. The words washed over him and there was a feeling of calm and peace in the room. When I stopped, though his eyes were closed, he squeezed my hand as if willing me to continue. I picked up the closest book, an aged copy of *My Utmost for His Highest,* and turned to a devotion in the middle. He listened intently and when I closed the book in fatigue, he reached out again and took my hand.

"You like it when I read, don't you?" My eyes were tired and burning, but I was not about to squander the chance of a response from him after watching him all day. So I closed my eyes and began the routine he had performed with me when I was little. "Once upon a time there was a boy who wanted to change the world. Many people who lived before him had tried to change the world, people who built bridges and flying machines and ran companies and countries and did great things, wonderful things, but never really changed the world the way he wanted to change it.

"So the boy decided he would follow God, and he listened closely and carefully to what God told him to do. And do you know what he heard God telling him? 'The power is in the Word.' He remembered the verses that say, 'The Word of God is alive and powerful. It is sharper than the sharpest two-edged sword, cutting between soul and spirit, between joint and marrow. It exposes our innermost thoughts and desires.'

"The boy devoted his life to the words that can change the world. Words that can change the heart. He took the words on the pages of the Bible and words from people who lived in the jungle and exchanged them. And the people had never seen such a thing. But when they began to read, something wonderful happened. One by one, hearts changed, and there was mercy and forgiveness and grace. And that's how the boy changed the world."

My father was asleep, breathing rhythmically, his stomach rising and falling like a newborn's. I sat back in the chair and started to pray, something else he had done with me as a child. I prayed for the people we had known in the jungle, the names of those I remembered. I prayed for other missionaries and extended family members he would know. I prayed for the president and members of Congress and governors, just as my father taught me, even though he had big differences with most political leaders. My voice grew softer in this audience with God and my father. And the longer I spoke, the more my prayer became a whisper and my heart turned toward my daughter.

"Oh, Lord, you know the struggles that Treha has been through. You know that her life is not easy, that the things she has seen and experienced have scarred her, and yet I believe you are good and that all of these things can work together for her and our eventual good. Would you encourage her in her studies tonight? Would you come alongside her and help her understand you better, understand your will for her life? And, Lord, would you give me the strength to show her that she does have a mother who cares, that she does have a grandfather and grandmother who love her? Give me the opening I need to reach her. Give me the courage I need."

I prayed so hard, concentrating on the inner image of Treha's face, that I didn't feel the movement beside me. I heard bedsprings creak and looked up to see my father leaning over me, eyes wide-open. He startled me and I jerked back, but when I looked more closely, I saw his mouth moving. He was trying to get words out but couldn't.

"What is it, Dad?"

There was pleading in his eyes, tears, but I couldn't reach him. No matter what I said, he was locked away. I whispered encouragement, trying to coax him out of the shell, to no avail.

Finally I stretched out a hand and caressed his stubble-covered face. "Do you want me to pray for you? Is that what you want, Dad? Do you want me to read to you again? I didn't even know you could hear me, but I'm glad you're here. I'm glad we can be together again."

His eyes begged in the muted light and the struggle continued. Then, exhausted, he sat back on the bed and let his arms dangle. I gently lowered his head to the pillow and he drew his legs to himself in a fetal position.

I returned to the Bible and read him Psalm 23. " 'The Lord is my shepherd; I have all that I need.' "

As I did, I recalled the letter I had written to my father shortly before Treha's birth. I hoped the letter had reached him, but I was never sure. We never talked about it, simply moved on, one foot in front of the other and no looking back.

" 'He lets me rest in green meadows; he leads me beside peaceful streams. He renews my strength. He guides me along right paths, bringing honor to his name.' "

I apologized to my father in that letter for letting him down, for letting God down. For my failure.

" 'Even when I walk through the darkest valley, I will not be afraid, for you are close beside me. Your rod and your staff protect and comfort me.' "

I'd told my father what I planned to name my daughter and that I hoped she would carry that name with her the rest of her life as a memorial. That one day I hoped to find her doing well and following God. And that perhaps one day he would meet her.

" 'You prepare a feast for me in the presence of my enemies. You honor me by anointing my head with oil. My cup overflows with blessings.' "

Things came back to me in that night watch. Memories and thoughts stirred by the mere presence of my family. Hopes and dreams that had been muted like my father's condition.

" 'Surely your goodness and unfailing love will pursue me all the days of my life, and I will live in the house of the Lord forever.' "

The next morning my mother was anxious to hear how things had gone. I told her Dad hadn't moved the rest of the night until first light when I was awakened by him sitting up and trying to get out of bed. I'd helped him to the bathroom.

When he was settled in front of the TV, I pulled her aside. "Something else happened last night. It was almost as if he was trying to tell me something or responding to something I said."

She asked what I had said and I ticked off the things I had read him but told her that I felt it was during my prayer that he became somewhat coherent. That's when he had gotten in my face.

"Mom, have you ever considered that maybe he was reacting to you in some way when he pushed you? When he became aggressive? Maybe he understands more than we're giving him credit for."

"I want to believe you're right, but you haven't seen him like I have."

"Take me back. What was going on that day?"

"I was talking to him. Our little running

conversation. Nothing out of the ordinary."

"What about? Politics? Sports? Did it have anything to do with me?"

Sometimes it pays to observe because at the moment I asked the question, my mother looked away. "Maybe you can remember every conversation, but I can't. Not at my age."

"Mom, please. Try."

She dried the dishes while we talked and it looked like she was doing extra duty on the water droplets. I let her clean, just standing there until she turned and saw me staring at her.

"I have a question for you," my mother said, her mouth flat and inexpressive. "If you tell your daughter, will you help her contact her father's family?"

"I haven't crossed that bridge yet."

The words fell in the space between us and were swallowed by the past and all we had done to make it go away.

Chapter 19

Treha

Treha put Cameron's card in his mailbox and hoped Shelly's anger would subside. But that didn't happen. The girl moved out of their room and slept on a friend's floor down the hall the first night.

Jill tried to keep things calm but Shelly had gone to the administration, which set off a formal complaint protocol that brought Treha in front of a counselor she had never met, Mrs. Tanholme.

The woman asked Treha a few questions about school and how classes were going, then got to the meat of the problem.

"She hasn't liked me from the first day," Treha said. "I think she wanted a different roommate. So I've tried to stay out of her way."

"Is that why you took the note from her and opened it?"

"I didn't take the note from her."

"Did you write the note yourself, Treha?"

"No."

"Then who did?"

"I've explained this. It was someone interested in Shelly who gave me the card. He thought I could help him get to know her. I was upset that he didn't like me, so I threw it in the trash. And when I thought about it and decided I'd made a mistake, it was gone. Shelly took it from my trash can."

"Why didn't you just tell him no, that you didn't want to give her the card?"

"I don't know. I couldn't think that fast."

"And you opened the card because . . . ?"

"I wanted to see what he wrote. I wanted him to say those things to me, and then I got angry."

Mrs. Tanholme nodded. "I understand. That must have been a little traumatic."

"I shouldn't have gotten my hopes up about a boyfriend."

"Why is that?"

"Because no one would want to be my boyfriend."

"Oh, Treha, I don't think that's true. What was it about this boy that interested you?"

"I don't know. I just liked him. He talked to me."

"Where did you meet him?"

"He's a student here."

"Treha, why don't you just tell us who the boy is? We won't embarrass him."

"I promised him I wouldn't tell."

"You're in trouble. Surely he would help you."

"I try to always keep my promises."

The woman came from behind her desk and sat beside Treha. "I know coming here has been a big transition. This year has been filled with changes. And since you've come from a difficult background, it's hard to integrate into a new social network. I'd hate to see anything like this derail your education."

"What do you mean, derail?"

"I mean these accusations. The questions. They hang over you and your studies. Cause stress. And you have enough of that already."

"The answer is simple. Shelly doesn't want me as a roommate. She's moved out. Things should go better now for both of us."

"I'm afraid Shelly isn't going to let this stop at a different room assignment. She's told us some other things that have us concerned."

"What things?"

"She said some of your class assignments weren't really yours."

"That's not true. I haven't handed in

anything that wasn't my own work."

"Let's just get this card issue behind us first. Give me a name so I can go in confidence and speak with him."

Treha thought a moment. "I made a promise. If I went back on it, who would be able to trust me? How could you trust what I say?"

"Would you be willing to ask him to talk with me?"

"I could try."

"Good. Excellent. I'll take that." She handed Treha a business card with her phone number on it. "Have him call me or stop by the office. The sooner the better. Okay?"

Treha walked through the halls and felt every eye on her. She felt guilty. She found Cameron in the cafeteria at dinner that evening and sat a few tables away and tried to catch his eye. She waved once and thought he had seen her but wasn't sure. When he stood to leave, she followed.

"Can I talk with you?" she said.

"I'm kind of busy, Treha."

"It won't take long. I need your help, Cameron." Just saying his name was painful.

He dumped his trash, then followed her

to the back of the room.

"Shelly accused me of stealing. She found the card you wrote and said I stole it. Then she accused me of writing it."

"Writing it? She thinks you're in love with her?"

"She went to the administration. I'm in trouble with them."

Cameron closed his eyes and shook his head. "I knew it. I never should have given that to you. It was so dumb."

Treha handed him Mrs. Tanholme's card. "Can you call the counselor and tell her the truth? Or go to her office?"

He stared at the name. "Treha, I don't want Shelly to know. It's so embarrassing. If she finds out I'm the one who actually wrote it, I'll get laughed out of school."

"The worst that happens is she's flattered by what you wrote but isn't interested."

"That's easy for you to say. That's not the worst that can happen. I mean, I appreciate you not telling anyone. I do. You kept your word. But I don't want her knowing."

"The counselor said you could just talk with her in confidence. You don't have to —"

"I'd like to help but I can't." Cameron walked away from her and through the double doors.

Treha returned to her empty room. Shelly's things had been moved. No more needing to go to the commons each morning. She could stay and work at her own desk. She moved it next to the window on Shelly's side, the one Shelly had claimed for herself before Treha arrived. She looked out the window at the changing color of the leaves and thought this felt like a new beginning. Or the beginning of the end.

CHAPTER 20

Paige

After a late-night flight on Sunday, I got through my Monday classes at Millhaven and drove to Bethesda to grab something to eat in the commons. I picked at my meal, searching for Treha but not finding her in the trickle of students that passed.

I should have called her, should have invited her to dinner. Should have bought a plane ticket for Tucson as soon as I'd seen the documentary. After all the lost time and delays and interruptions, I didn't want to squander another day without my daughter knowing, no matter what the consequences.

I usually try to be fashionably on time for class, not too early, not too late, but I couldn't help rushing there tonight. I didn't want to embarrass Treha; that wouldn't be fair. We needed to be alone when she found out, but I just wanted to see her. Talk to her.

The class filled. The clock ticked. Treha's seat remained empty. I welcomed the students and stalled, checking the door every thirty seconds. I mentioned that I had been out of town for a few days and went into a devotional about my father and the legacy of words. When my voice caught, I switched emotional gears and rehearsed his career as a translator, the safe parts of his story that I could speak through without weeping.

Finally I checked the roll and asked if anyone had seen Treha, and from the back came a timid hand. "I think something's going on in her dorm."

"What do you mean?"

"I saw a security guard and the RA in her room."

I knew I had to continue the class, that I couldn't abandon them, but I also couldn't abandon Treha. I had prepared a writing prompt for the end of class but quickly pulled it out and put it on the screen and gave them a timed assignment. Some looked confused but I told them I needed to leave for a few minutes, then hurried toward her dorm.

The door was locked, but a student at the desk buzzed me in.

"I'm looking for Treha Langsam's room. Do you know her?"

The girl's eyes widened. "Yeah, but she's not there. They took her to the admin building."

I rushed there and made it as far as the security office. There was a flurry of activity in an office that should have been quiet this time of night. The young man at the front asked if he could help me, but I saw D. C. behind him and got his attention.

"I'm looking for one of my students, Treha Langsam."

"She's here, ma'am. There's been an incident at her dorm."

"What kind of incident?"

"We're waiting on the dean."

"What happened?"

Treha looked through the open door of D. C.'s office, her eyes red and puffy. My heart melted. I wanted to envelop her and never let her go. "I need to see her."

"I'm not sure that's the best idea, ma'am."

I tried to speak, tried to come up with words that would convince him or at least to communicate with my eyes. Finally D. C. nodded and I walked past him and closed the door behind me.

"I'm sorry I'm not in class," Treha said. Her fingers were moving on her lap as if she were typing out her defense without a keyboard.

"Treha, what happened?"
"They came into my room."
"Who?"
"The RA, Jill. And the security people. They went to my closet and lifted up some of my clothes and found some jewelry. I guess it was Shelly's. A necklace and some earrings."
"They're saying you took them?"
"Yes."
"Did you?"
"No. I've never seen them before."
It sounded like a setup, and the bile rose in my throat. It would be a case of she-said, she-said. And who would believe a loner like Treha?
"I just want to go back to Arizona. I don't belong here."
"I'm sure it's a misunderstanding."
"She was upset with me about the card she found, too."
"What card?"
Treha described the prior conflict with Shelly. Searching for something to say, something that felt right, I sat beside her. "It's not true that you don't belong. You do."
"How would you know that?"
"I've been around schools and students long enough to know. Trust me. Don't give

up just because life has gotten a little difficult."

"A little?"

"A lot."

She looked like a fish out of water, scooting forward on the chair and rubbing her hands against her jeans. How anyone could mistreat someone like Treha was beyond me.

"I want to call my friend. Do I get a phone call?"

"You're not being arrested. You can call anyone you want."

I got out my cell phone and handed it to Treha. She waved me off and said she had her own. But before she could dial, D. C. walked in.

"I'm supposed to take you up to see the dean."

"D. C., this is a setup," I said. "Surely you can see that. How did you find out about the missing items in the first place?"

"Her roommate told her RA that some items were missing. She came in one day earlier in the week and startled Treha. She was hiding something, acting strange. And she thought she saw her hiding something under her clothes."

"That's not true," Treha said.

"I'm telling you what we were told."

"I want to go home," Treha said, her eyes

vacant, the fingers typing again.

"Come with me, Treha," D. C. said.

"Can I go with you?" I heard myself say.

D. C. shrugged.

"Aren't you teaching the class?" Treha said.

"I'm fine. This is more important."

I stood and followed them to the elevator and we rode to the top floor. The carpet was so thick I nearly lost my shoes. Along the hallway were pictures of school presidents and members of the board. Understated furniture, but not too understated. I had been to this floor twice as a student and it looked basically the same. D. C. led us to a conference room where the dean of students, Jared Douglas, waited. I knew Jared from our student days. He was also one of Ron Gleason's best friends.

"Paige, I didn't expect to see you," Jared said. He was a wiry man with glasses, impeccably dressed. Even at this time of night his tie was perfect and his shirt still creased from the last ironing.

"Well, these are extraordinary circumstances," I said. "I wanted to make sure Treha has a chance to tell her side of the story."

"I see." He gestured toward the open seats and looked at his file. "Treha, you signed an agreement at the beginning of the year. A code of conduct. Do you remember that?"

"Yes. And I haven't broken it."

"If we find otherwise, it's an immediate dismissal. And you forfeit the money that's been paid for the semester. So I urge you to consider this carefully." He glanced at me and it was all I could do to not respond. "Everyone makes mistakes. There's certainly forgiveness for what you may have done, but there are also consequences. When a case is brought against a student like this —"

"Jared, could I see you in the hall a minute?" I said, an edge to my voice. He acted as if I'd just tossed a dead fish into his manila folder, but he finally nodded, and when he'd closed the massive door and we stood in the carpet that was as deep as a snowfall, he pushed back.

"Paige, I'm all for teachers taking an interest in their students, but I don't understand why you're inserting yourself into this."

"The girl is alone. She has no advocate. Shelly's family has a lot of pull with the administration. You know that. All things being equal, she's the one they'll believe."

"If you're suggesting we play favorites, you're wrong. I resent that insinuation. We're capable of handling this fairly and without favoritism."

"I'm not calling your judgment into question. I just don't think she needs — just listen to her side of the story."

"I'll do that. I'm getting to that."

"She needs to know someone believes in her. She didn't do anything wrong."

His brows knit together and made his forehead crease like an old map. "And how do you know this? I have her RA and the head of security and a student who used to be her roommate and some missing jewelry. How could you possibly know if she's stolen something or not?"

There are some things a mother knows. The words tried to rise up from deep inside me but I held them back and instead put a hand on his arm. "Please. All I'm asking is that you would hear her side."

He nodded but clearly wanted to ask more. I opened the door and quickly moved to the table. Jared sat and folded his hands over the file and asked Treha to give her side of the story. I expected a tear-filled, jittery speech, but Treha was surprisingly calm and collected, though she did type with her fingers on the table in front of her as she spoke.

She explained what had happened from the first day. Jared listened and asked follow-up questions about the jewelry. The note that Shelly had found was another damning piece of evidence but Treha answered that with aplomb. She didn't give the identity of the author, but as she described the event, it was clear this wasn't some rehearsed speech but the truth.

"All right, I think I have enough information to go on," Jared said. "You've been helpful, Treha, and I'm sorry you've been put through this."

"Does that mean you believe her?" I said.

"That means I have more fact-finding to do. I want to talk with the other parties."

"You can see she's telling the truth," I said.

"There are some serious questions we need to deal with. Sometimes you need the wisdom of Solomon to sort out such things."

"And sometimes you just need a little common sense. And resolve." I glanced at the clock. "Treha, our class is still in session. Should we go?"

Her eyes were moving now as she stared at the table in front of her. "I don't know if I can go back to the class. They all think I'm a liar."

"Nonsense. Most of them have no idea about this. You can't let what other people think dictate your life."

I stood and waited to see what Treha

would do. After a few seconds, she got up and followed me to the elevator.

CHAPTER 21

Treha

Treha stood a little closer to Ms. Redwine as the elevator doors closed. It felt good to have someone believe her story and take her side. She hadn't experienced that since being with Miriam and Elsie in Arizona.

"This young man who wrote the card to Shelly," Ms. Redwine said. "Is he cute?"

The question surprised Treha. "Extremely," she said.

"Really? What is your definition of extremely cute?" There was a smile to her question and when Treha didn't answer, she asked another. "I mean, is it the way he looks, his eyes, his muscles, or something intangible?"

"It's everything. The way he looks and the way he acts. He noticed me."

Treha thought she saw tears in the woman's eyes, but Ms. Redwine looked away and quickly resumed the conversation.

"Well, it sounds like he chose to use you to get to Shelly. I'm sorry that happened. Obviously extreme cuteness does not automatically give one discernment."

"I liked that he talked with me."

"That is a good start to a relationship, isn't it?"

They crossed campus and just before they entered the classroom, Ms. Redwine stopped and turned. "Treha, you're probably wondering why I went with you to that meeting."

She nodded. "You can't do that for all of your students or you would never teach a class."

"Right. But you're not just any student. You're one of a kind." The woman bit her lower lip. "Could we go for coffee or something after class? I'd like to talk more."

Treha considered this. She had an empty room to return to in the dorm. She also had an empty stomach and she felt alone. Just the possibility of another person to talk with sounded wonderful. Especially someone who had treated her kindly.

"I'd like that," Treha said.

Walking into the classroom with all the people looking at her wasn't quite as difficult when walking in with Ms. Redwine. The teacher apologized to the other students for taking longer than the timed writing assignment, then launched into the lesson.

"There's a reason why I chose fear as the topic of your writing prompt. As a writer this is something you must attack and wrestle. When you give voice to your fear, when you expose it, as vulnerable as that makes you, you give others the same permission. You give them courage to believe there's more to life than cowering. You give hope. And my guess is, when you tackle your inner fears, you will eventually tackle what's holding you back from who God intended you to be. Your fears lead you to who you really are."

Ms. Redwine's voice cracked and Treha noticed she was staring straight at her. The teacher composed herself, turned toward the front screen, and said to the class, "So who's brave enough to tell me what they wrote about?"

Silence in the classroom, but eventually students began to raise their hands. They talked about fears of failure, of not doing well in school, of letting down their professors or their parents or God. Treha listened intently but kept her eyes on her desktop.

"This is all very good," Ms. Redwine said. "To write is to be vulnerable. To be willing to learn more than you wanted about your fears. About yourself."

A student near the back of the room raised his hand. "What would you have written about, Ms. Redwine? What is your fear?"

Treha looked up in surprise. She wondered if the teacher would answer the question.

Ms. Redwine stared at the student, then at the floor, rubbing her hands and tapping a pen against her thigh. "That's a good question." She moved to the desk and leaned against it. "My fear . . ." She chuckled. "Maybe I should have spent time writing this down."

"It's okay if you don't want to talk about —"

"No, that's all right. Thank you for the question. It's fair to push those who try to teach you. I've just come from my parents' home in Florida, where things have pretty much fallen apart, so I'm a little emotional. My father is older now. He has a disease. Years ago he called it 'old-timer's,' but it's not so funny anymore."

She looked at her hands, then studied the pen closely. "My answer to this question might have been different a few years ago. It might have even been different a few days ago. But that's the thing with God. He uses circumstances, struggles, to do things in us.

"My fear was that because of past mistakes and failure, I was less than usable to him. I've been living under the belief that I have to impress him, that I have to make every right choice from now on. That I've used up his grace, and one more mistake and I'm through. So my fear has held me back from trying.

"I've been working on a thesis for years. I had a sabbatical and it nearly killed me because I tried to put down my ideas, but every time I looked at my notes, I couldn't. I was afraid. Now I think the fear wasn't about writing the wrong thing. It wasn't about not getting it right. It was about disclosure. Unveiling and letting others see."

"What's your thesis?" another student asked.

"It's about mothers and daughters in literature. Healing strained relationships between parent and child."

Treha wondered if that was why Ms. Redwine had asked questions about her mother, because of her thesis. The woman seemed genuine, but was she trying to use Treha for her writing, as Anna had done?

Ms. Redwine glanced at the clock. "I think that's enough for tonight. We can end a few minutes early." She gave the next assignment and dismissed them. And as the class filed out, she asked Treha to join her in the commons for the coffee they'd talked about.

Treha hesitated for a second, then nodded.

Chapter 22

Paige

There were tables and chairs strewn about the commons, ghosts of conversations past. The smell of brewed coffee lingered. Students talked or studied or both.

I chose a booth along the side, behind a pillar I thought would give us privacy. As I placed my things on the bench, I wondered what to say and how to say it, wondered how Treha would respond. I sat down across from her, feeling as though the question from class still hung in the air. *What is your fear?* The part of me that wanted to stay hidden, the part that made my heart want to beat out of my chest and run and hide and retreat, would not win tonight.

Treha sat too and looked at the tabletop.

"Treha, I have something I need to tell you." When she didn't look up, I opened my purse. "You showed me a letter from your mother. I'm sorry; I didn't mean to take the copy with me."

Treha looked up at me. "Do you want to use my story in your thesis? Is that why you're talking to me?"

"What do you mean?"

"My story is just like the paper you're writing. The relationship between mothers and daughters in stories."

"Oh. No, this isn't about my dissertation." I held the letter out, my hands shaking. "I've written one good essay from the heart in my life, and I've lived in fear that someone would discover I wrote it. But I've also lived with a hope that you would be that person."

Treha searched my eyes, hers filled with confusion. I reached out and touched her hand. "I remember the night you were born. I remember your first cry. It broke my heart when they took you away." Tears formed but I didn't push them away. "I remember the smell of the hospital. I remember it was raining when they took me to my room. I asked if I could see you. They said I couldn't. That if I saw you, I'd want to keep you. I promised I wouldn't. I begged to hold you."

I fought the tears and a whisper escaped through the broken places of my heart. "Treha, you're my daughter."

Her voice was flat, not questioning but

stating. "You're my mother."

I could feel the distance between us and tried to close it with words.

"I should have told you. I should have come looking for you. I was afraid. I've watched you here, read your essays. I've fallen in love with you. Again."

Treha's fingers began to move on the tabletop and I heard noise around us, behind us, but I focused on her. I was desperate to ask her questions, to embrace her, but I held back, trying to wait for her to be ready. We sat for several minutes, not speaking, just me looking at my daughter, her looking at me. I wiped away tears but Treha had none.

Finally Treha said, "Elsie told me this would happen. She believed I would meet my mother."

"Elsie was right."

"I have so many questions," Treha said.

The whispers behind me had grown louder and I glanced back at a group of students in the next booth. They quickly dropped their eyes to the table or their phones. My heart sank. Were they close enough to have heard us?

I turned back to Treha. "Let's go somewhere else."

CHAPTER 23

Treha

Treha tried to look into the eyes of her mother, tried to see some reflection of herself. Ms. Redwine was beautiful. Her face looked nothing like Treha's — she had a smooth complexion, thin lips, silky-smooth hair. Her eyes didn't move and she looked like she'd never struggled with weight.

Ms. Redwine drove off campus, and they found an IHOP a few miles away.

"You knew it was me because of my name, didn't you?" Treha said once they'd ordered. "Your letter said that was how you'd know."

"Yes. I always thought one day I would read a story about you, this girl with the strange name. You'd be quoted in a newspaper article after discovering a cure for some exotic disease."

"But I haven't."

Ms. Redwine smiled. "You don't have to

cure anything. You're my daughter."

Their food arrived and Treha sat in silence, adding butter and moving it around her pancakes with a bent fork. Ms. Redwine leaned forward. "What is it, Treha? What are you thinking?"

"Are you sure?"

"About what?"

"That you're her. There are others who have told me I'm their daughter."

"Treha —"

"You don't look like me."

"We can have a DNA test, but that's my letter you've been carrying. And you have my father's eyes."

Treha stared at her. "Really?"

"The color is uncanny."

"My grandparents. Do they know about me? That you found me?"

"My mother does. My father has been struggling with dementia. Alzheimer's. But I'm sure if he were aware that I'd found you, he would want to give you a big hug."

"What about your mother?"

"My mother . . . she would love you too. It was hard for her when I got pregnant. She was upset and felt betrayed. She had waited so long to become pregnant after she and my father got married. And there I was, a teenager, having a baby."

"How did you feel?"

"Ashamed. A million pounds of guilt. I didn't want to let my parents down. Especially my father. When they decided I should fly back to have you — from the mission field, where I grew up — I felt it was best."

"And to give me up for adoption."

Ms. Redwine's brow creased. "I thought I was placing you in the loving hands of someone who could give you a good life. Obviously, that didn't happen."

"Did you have brothers or sisters?"

"I'm an only child."

"Like me."

"Yes."

"I might be able to help your father. Sometimes, at Desert Gardens, I could help the residents."

Ms. Redwine put down her coffee. "I would like you to meet him, but I don't want you to feel pressure. I didn't tell you this so you would fix my father. You're under no obligation —"

"What if I want to help him?"

"If that's what you want." She patted Treha's hand a little awkwardly. There was a buzz in the woman's purse but she ignored it and took another sip of coffee.

Treha had been ravenously hungry in class, but now she could hardly think of food. “I met Dr. Crenshaw. He was your doctor, wasn’t he?”

“Yes.” She sat back, her eyes dropping to the table. “In the last few months of the pregnancy I became depressed. It was overwhelming. I believed what he said, that the medication wouldn’t affect you. And I was in so much pain . . . If only I hadn’t taken that. Your life would have been different.”

“He felt guilty too,” Treha said. “We looked through his files after he died. I thought maybe we would find a clue about you, but we didn’t. The pastor who worked on the adoption had died. I gave up on ever finding you.”

“Then you came here.”

“Because of Elsie. She’s the one who suggested Bethesda.”

“Thank God for Elsie,” Ms. Redwine said. “You could have gone anywhere in the country. But you came here. Can you believe it, Treha? That we’re together?”

The butter had melted into the pancakes, wet and glistening yellow. Treha poured a dribble of syrup and let it soak. “Why did you wait so long?”

Ms. Redwine took a deep breath. “I wish I hadn’t. I was . . . stuck. Have you ever felt that way? That you simply can’t move?”

Treha nodded.

"I hope you can forgive me."

Treha looked down. "I don't know you," she muttered.

The woman cradled her coffee mug with both hands. "Treha, I made a good choice in having you. I believed you would be raised in a loving home and that the only person who would hurt was me. I prayed for you and believed the best. Every year when your birthday rolled around, I would imagine cake and presents, friends coming to your house. I envied your teachers. I wondered what you were reading."

Another buzz in her purse.

"Do you want to answer that?"

"I suppose I should make sure it's not my mother. . . ." Ms. Redwine picked up the phone. "No, it's . . . not." She turned the phone off and put it back in her purse.

"Who was it?"

"Another professor. I'll call him back later."

"Is he your friend?"

"Ron is . . . yes, he's a friend," she said, her lips tightening. "Treha, I don't ask you to understand. I don't even know that it's fair to ask your forgiveness for not reaching out sooner. I think all I'm asking you is that you give me a chance."

"To make it up to me?"

"No. To be your mother. To be something I wanted to be but couldn't."

Treha took a small bite of the darkened part of her pancakes and then a sip of orange juice.

"I want to help you through this situation, your roommate's accusations. I want to help you be everything God wants you to be. I have so much hope for your future. For us."

"Are you sure that you want me? Even though I'm like this?"

"Of course."

"Maybe that's the reason you didn't find me. Maybe you don't want someone with my problems."

"Everyone has problems. The bigger question is whether you'll want *me.* And I will understand if you say no."

Treha took another bite of pancake. She chewed slowly, swallowed, then said, "I'm ready to hear about him."

"Him?"

"My father."

A deep breath and the woman sat back. "Your father. All right, what would you like to know?"

"Did you get married?"

A shadow passed over Ms. Redwine's face

and Treha couldn't help but feel sorry for her.

"No. I would have liked that."

"Did he ask you?"

"We were young. We made promises we couldn't keep. We pledged to always love each other. He said he would return with a ring. He didn't."

"Where is he?"

She shifted in her seat. "He died, Treha. Shortly after he returned to school, a few months later. My parents got word of a car accident. Icy Colorado roads. It was tragic."

Treha felt as though a door had slammed shut in the corridor of her life, one she'd never really known was open. She had always wondered about her mother. Her mother was the one she had longed for, searched for. But now that she had found her, she wanted to meet him, as well. And now she would never see him or hear his voice . . . "Were you sad?"

"I was numb for a while. It felt like it was happening to someone else. And the secrecy — we kept my pregnancy from everyone at the mission. Pretended I was just going away to school."

"What was he like?"

Ms. Redwine smiled. "Handsome. Athletic. Intelligent. I loved his voice. It was like listening to a direct link to his soul when he talked."

"Did you love him?"

"I thought I did. I thought we were made for each other. But I was seventeen. Almost eighteen. I didn't know anything, really.

"We met early in the summer the year before you were born. He came to work with the mission on a short-term trip. He was with a group working in the village, doing building projects and vacation Bible school. They played sports with the kids on the beach, but they needed an interpreter. I grew up there and knew the language. That's how we met. I was infatuated immediately. I couldn't stop thinking about him. But I was naive and so inexperienced at love. I knew if my parents found out, they'd put a stop to it, so I kept it a secret."

"Was he in love with you?"

"I thought so. Maybe he just saw me as exotic, growing up in the jungle. He really had a heart to serve God; we talked about that a lot."

"But he wasn't telling the truth?"

"I think he was sincere. Our passion just got out of hand."

Treha put her fork down. "What was it like? To kiss a boy?"

"You do have a lot of questions, don't

you?" Ms. Redwine stifled a laugh. "I think it was better than I imagined. It felt forbidden and yet natural. I hadn't watched lots of movies or read romance novels, so I didn't have a lot of preconceived notions. And I learned that once the engine of passion starts, it's hard not to rev it. Does that make sense?"

Treha nodded.

"Well, I begged God to forgive me. I promised I wouldn't let it happen again. But we kept meeting. He felt ashamed and guilty like I did. But then it would happen again."

"What was his name?"

"David. David Weber."

Treha rolled the name around in her mind. *David.* Her father's name was David. "What did he say when he found out you were pregnant?"

"He never found out."

Treha's mouth dropped. "What? He didn't know about me?"

Another pained look from Ms. Redwine. "He left late in the summer and promised to write, to come back soon. But my parents discovered the pregnancy and felt it best to keep it to ourselves, have the baby, and move on with life."

"And you agreed."

The woman's cheeks flushed. "I was mortified. I felt so guilty. I didn't want to hurt them any more than I already had."

"In your letter, you said you trusted someone with your heart, and he wasn't trustworthy."

Ms. Redwine looked down at her hands. "I did say that. Looking back, it probably wasn't fair. I was so young. . . . He did write to me like he promised. I received two letters. My parents read both of them, then gave them to me. He told me he loved me, that he wanted to spend the rest of his life with me, and he hoped we would eventually get married. But I could tell with the second letter that something had changed, like he was having second thoughts. Then came the news that he had been killed."

"Did you ever visit his grave? Go see his parents?"

"No. The last twenty years have been a long climb up a hill of regret and shame. I've tried to forget, but the past returns like a boomerang. A good boomerang, Treha. I'm so glad to have found you. I know this is not going to be easy, moving forward. I know you're going to have questions and it will be hard, but I also think it's going to be good. For both of us."

"Do you have a picture of him?"

Ms. Redwine's chin puckered a little and she nodded. "I have one I saved in a memory book. I'll get it down and show you."

"Tomorrow?" Treha said.

"Sure."

Treha paused, trying to sort through the jumble of questions in her mind. "What do I call you?"

"That's a good question. What do you want to call me?"

"I don't know. It doesn't feel right to call you Ms. Redwine, but it doesn't feel right to call you Mother or Mom either."

The woman nodded. "You can call me Paige, if that's easier. But let's take our time. When the moment is right, you'll know what to call me."

Treha pushed the syrup around on her pancakes. This was the moment she had waited for all her life. To sit with her mother and talk. To learn the truth. To *be* with her mother. She couldn't figure out why she had a bad feeling. Or maybe why she had no feeling at all.

CHAPTER 24

Paige

I dropped Treha off at her dorm just before curfew, got out, and hugged her. She did not return the hug, per se, but I felt a slight movement of her hands toward my back. I gave her my cell number and asked her to call me in the morning.

Once she'd disappeared inside, the clunk of the electronic lock securing her, I sat in the parking lot in the aftermath. Everything had changed in one evening. Everything had come into the open, and what should have been the greatest feeling of relief felt more like a new cloud.

When I was pregnant, when I had a more romanticized view of life, I had dreamed of this moment, dreamed of what we would talk about, where we might go and how the story might spill out. The look in her eyes as I told her. I could have taken her back to my home, and we could have stayed up all night looking at pictures and laughing, filling the blank spaces of her history, but this was not Treha's way. I sensed we needed to ease into things.

How was I to go about this? I had no earthly idea how to be a mother, no pattern set before me other than my own mother and the mothers whose stories I had read. Ma Ingalls and Marmee March and the weak, feckless mothers of Dickens or conniving and conflicted mothers like Hamlet's Gertrude. Maybe I could become more like Marilla to Anne?

I checked my phone and saw that Ron Gleason had left a text. And a voice mail. The text said, Please call me. He had sent an e-mail while I had visited my mother and father, detailing the things he was praying for me and how much he hoped God would sustain me. I'd written a brief response, telling him I appreciated his kindness. I did appreciate it, but I hoped the brevity of the e-mail would communicate that I still needed space.

I retrieved my messages and listened to the slight rasp in his voice, a little strained from the usual composed, self-assured tone.

"Paige, I just saw a video post from a Bethesda student on Facebook. I'm stunned. Is this true? Can you call me?" He took a breath and in my mind I could see him searching for words. "I suppose if it is, you're probably speaking with her right now, your daughter. Wow. That's hard to imagine. For me. And for you, probably. Sorry. It must be amazing for you to find her. For both of you. So I guess I'll try not to bother you. But I . . . I wanted you to know —"

I hit Pause on the message. What was he talking about? What video?

I let the message play again.

"I wanted you to know this doesn't change anything . . . for me. We all have things in the past. Regrets. Mistakes. I have those. A trunkful. I can handle anything else that's in there. I'm a little shocked, I guess, but if it's true, I want you to know I'm here. If you need someone to talk with . . . please call."

My heart raced, my breath short. If Ron had seen this video online, which somehow told him Treha was my daughter, who else had seen it? It was hard enough to deal with my revelation and how Treha would react without worrying about social media backlash. And then I thought of Ron. He must have wondered why I hadn't shared this dark secret. He was not part of my inner circle of confidants.

Poor Ron. How could anyone compare with a memory that only enhances with years? I had held David in my mind. He was forever young, stuck at the same age, with strength in his body and no flab. His hair would never recede. His smile would always be the same, locked in the prison of my memory.

I drove too fast, and once home, I checked Facebook but couldn't find anything about Treha and me. How had Ron discovered it? I dialed his number but got his voice mail. I hung up before leaving a message.

I went to my closet and pulled down the albums, the dusty past, and turned the browned and weathered pages until I came to the one that took my breath away. My mother had taken the photos. The two of us had been working with the children that day, and she wanted to get us in action for the next prayer letter. One shot was of the team playing on the beach — but the one I treasured was David with his arm around my shoulder, pulling me close, smiling. Both of us smiling so wide, unable to help it.

I pulled the photo from behind the plastic cover and held it there. Such a long time ago. Such a different life, a different world. I placed the photo in my purse and left the albums on the floor.

I tried Ron again, but there was no answer. "Ron, it's Paige. Thanks for your message — please call me when you get this."

I changed for bed and pulled my well-worn journal from the nightstand. I wrote in it infrequently, making a halfhearted attempt to record my life, to chronicle milestones and observations. But tonight words poured out about Treha, my fears, my questions about the future. I was lost in writing until a knock at the front door shocked me. I put on my robe, tied it, and walked barefoot across the hardwood. The security light had come on outside and I saw the outline of a man. Ron.

I unlocked the door and he smiled and nodded, ducking his head apologetically.

"Ron . . . what are you doing here?"

"Paige, I'm sorry it's late. I just had the sense that I needed to come over."

He held out a hand, asking permission to enter, and I opened the door wider. "Sure. Did you get my message?"

"No. I left the house without my phone."

He stood in the entry until I ushered him inside.

"Can you show me where you saw the video?"

"Get your computer."

He navigated to Facebook and played the

video of my conversation with Treha in the Bethesda commons. I remembered the whispers in the booth behind us, my concern about being overheard, but it never occurred to me that they might've thought our conversation worth recording. It was like watching the most intimate moment of your life from a slightly different angle. So violating and invasive.

"Do you know the student who posted this?" I said.

"I don't, but if you don't want this displayed, I'll send a message now. And one to the student development office. We should be able to get it pulled pretty quickly."

"Yes, please."

Ron wrote a message from his own account to the student, then called the dean and spoke with him. My heart began to calm a little, believing someone was putting out the fire.

"He's going to handle it now — and said he would go to the dorm if he has to," Ron said, returning to the living room sofa.

I sat across from him on the love seat. "Thank you for this. I'm so glad you saw it."

"Paige, I can't imagine what it's been like, with what you've kept hidden, kept inside all these years. I don't know the particulars and I don't have to, but I assume this young lady really is your daughter."

"It's true."

His face was serious, lines of consternation in his forehead like he was in mental anguish. "Right."

"Okay, well . . . thank you," I said as compassionately as I could through my bewilderment.

"Doggone it, Paige, I want a relationship with you. I do." He said it quickly like he had finally decided on his drink order at Starbucks.

I didn't know how to respond. He seemed nervous, but I was just as undone. I tried to bring some levity to the situation. "I've never heard you say 'doggone it.' I didn't know it was in your vocabulary."

That got a small chuckle. "It's a minced oath. But it's true." He rubbed his hands together and sat forward, elbows on knees. "This other guy, is he the reason you're not sure about us? The reason you're not as sure as I am? Is he still in the picture?"

I stifled a smile. For as awkward as the whole thing was, it was equally sweet. "Ron, Treha's father died a long time ago."

He looked down. "Oh, I see. I'm sorry. I mean . . . I'm glad in one sense, from a selfish perspective, but I'm sorry for your loss."

"It was many years ago."

"And you weren't married?"

"No. I was a teenager. It was a very painful thing for my family and part of the reason I waited so long to find her. It's complicated, as all of my life seems to be now."

"And I don't need to hear it to say what I need to say to you. It's late and I've overstepped my boundaries, coming here and intruding. I just felt like . . ."

"Go ahead, Ron, you can speak freely."

"All right. Here's the thing, Paige. I know you have to figure things out with this young lady. But I want to be with you. I know it won't be easy. I know we have hurdles, but I believe we could be a really great team. Maybe even become a family."

My heart picked up speed and I struggled to keep my voice even and unemotional. I wanted to be in control of what I said. "That's kind of you, Ron. And thoughtful. I'm blown away that you were concerned for me . . . But I can't move in that direction yet. I honestly don't know if I can at all. This has nothing to do with you. . . . You're wonderful. And I would hate for any of this to interrupt our friendship. I think you can be a great role model for Treha, for example."

He nodded and winced like something had pierced his gut. Then he slapped his hands against his knees and said, "Fair enough. Well, I've taken up enough time." He stood and moved toward the door. "I'm sorry if I startled you."

I followed him to the door, searching desperately for something to say, something that would convey my heart. All I could come up with was, "I'm glad you came over, Ron."

He nodded again and closed the door behind him. I turned off the lights in the front room and watched from the shadows by the window as he pulled away.

Chapter 25

Treha

Treha sat in the commons in her regular booth, not having slept the entire night. She had tossed and turned and finally decided it was senseless to try any longer, so she got up, took a shower, and headed downstairs. She wanted to call Miriam in Arizona. She wanted to talk with Elsie and tell her she had been right, she had met her mother — at least she thought she had. But it was too early to call.

Instead she scribbled furiously in her journal, trying to capture everything. The sudden warmth she'd felt at Ms. Redwine's hug. The sincerity in the woman's face. How she had gone with Treha to face the dean of students. It was something a mother would have done for her daughter.

The minutes whirred by and the campus came to life, the sun rising on another day. Treha's head and body ached from lack of sleep. It wasn't until Anna sat down across from her that she looked up from the page.

"Holy cow. Hoo-ooly cow, Treha. Can you believe this? I mean, this is like a Pulitzer waiting to happen."

"What are you talking about?"

"Your story. Ms. Redwine's story. She's really your mother?"

"How did you know about that?"

"Uh . . . well, social media has this way of making things explode. Somebody was at the commons last night when Ms. Redwine . . . your mother . . . I can't get over that . . ."

"Somebody did what?"

"Here, I'll show you." Anna pulled out her phone. "The original post was taken down, but not before it got shared like a billion times." She played the video and Treha watched Ms. Redwine tell her the truth. Whoever took the video had been behind them and didn't capture her mother's face but showed Treha's face. As it ended, Treha noticed her fingers were typing on the tabletop. She folded her hands in her lap, trying to hold them still.

"So is she really your mom?"

"She says she is."

"Holy cow, Treha. This is what you've been waiting for! You have to do a piece for the paper. Better yet, let me do an interview."

"I don't want to be in the paper." She pushed the phone away. "I don't want everyone to see this. Can you stop it?"

Anna rolled her eyes. "That's like stopping a train. This thing has gone viral. Holy cow, Treha."

"Why do you keep saying that?"

"Because this is like the most dramatic thing that's ever happened here. It's a human interest story on steroids. You better get ready for the onslaught because there are going to be people coming out of the woodwork. Unless . . ."

"Unless what?"

"Unless you give somebody the story first."

"Like you."

"Hey, I'm just a friend who cares."

Treha looked hard at Anna.

"Okay, I'm just an opportunistic student who wants to be a reporter and wants the story first. I admit it. But here's the kicker. I do care about you. I care about this school and its reputation. You're not going to get that out there in the big, bad world."

Treha closed her journal and sat in silence. Her fingers started tapping on the journal cover and she didn't try to stop them.

"Treha, what's wrong?"

Treha got up and Anna grabbed her arm. "Tell me."

"I can't talk to you if you're going to write everything I say," Treha said.

Anna lifted both hands. "Fine. No pen. No recorder. Let's just talk. Totally off the record."

"I don't believe you. You promised me things before and went back on your word."

"You're right. And I apologized. This is your chance to let me try again."

Treha sat and stared at her. "I still don't think I can trust you."

"Treha, you need to talk. You have nobody else, right?"

"I have my friends in Arizona."

"They're a couple hours behind us." She put a hand over Treha's. "I'm not writing anything about this. I just want to be your friend."

Treha looked into the girl's eyes and the sight warmed her. There was something good and true there. Compassion. Kindness. Remorse.

"What happened with Shelly? I heard she was making a big stink."

Treha told her about the visit with the dean of students and how Ms. Redwine had shown up. "I was sure they were going to kick me out of school."

"They know you didn't take Shelly's stuff. That's crazy. Why would you want her jewelry? If you had stolen it, you wouldn't hide it in your room. The whole thing should get Shelly a one-way ticket home."

"She believed me."

"Who did?"

"Ms. Redwine. She spoke kindly about me and it felt really good to have someone on my side."

"Duh, Treha. She's your mother."

Treha didn't answer.

"Wait, don't you believe her? Treha, what possible reason could she have to lie about that? For crying out loud, she's risking her reputation."

"Something doesn't feel right."

"What do you mean?"

Treha hesitated, her head pounding now, and put a hand to her forehead. It felt like a migraine coming on, the old pain that used to send her over the edge. She tried to push it away, tried to get around the ache that spread and made it feel like her whole head was swelling to the point of bursting.

"Did you two talk more last night?" Anna said.

Treha nodded and then the whole thing came spilling out, like pancakes and syrup sliding off a plate.

"Holy cow," Anna said when she was done. "I can understand, after all you've been through, that you would be a little guarded. No, a lot guarded. But she knows too much for it to be a fraud."

"I don't think she's a fraud. I think she believes I'm her daughter. There's just something that . . ."

"Something that what?"

Treha searched for the words but couldn't find them. All her life she'd been fascinated with words, could handle jumbles and puzzles so easily, but now she had nothing. She shook her head.

Anna leaned closer. "What about your father?"

"I told you. He's dead."

"Right, but does he have any family? Parents?"

"I don't know." Treha looked down at the table. "I thought all I needed to know about was her. All I wanted was some connection to where I came from."

"And now that you have answers, you have more questions."

Treha nodded.

Anna thought a moment. "Maybe I can help."

"What do you mean?"

"Tell me what you know, about where they met and all of that. Where he was from. His name."

"I don't know much."

"You don't need to know much. Just names. Locations."

"She said she has a picture."

"Perfect. See if you can get that."

Chapter 26

Paige

Everyone who knew about the atomic bomb expected the destruction of Hiroshima and Nagasaki. Few expected the far-reaching fallout and the toll it took on history. I'd known moving toward my daughter would have repercussions. I didn't plan on the white-hot spotlight of social media.

The first indication, of course, was Ron showing up at my door in the middle of the night. Next came phone calls and voice mails from friends and colleagues, mostly positive and supportive. My mother called and left a message. But there was nothing from Treha. I wasn't sure if I should call her or not.

"I can't believe you've done this," my mother said when I returned her call on the way to school the next morning.

"How did you hear about it?" I said.

She mentioned a name from the past I

didn't recall, some connection from the mission whose daughter had seen something on Facebook and called with the news. The grapevine has gotten longer and the world is a much smaller place.

"Telling Treha this way was not something I planned, Mom. It just happened."

"Just like the way she was conceived, I'm sure."

The words were biting and angry, the mask giving way. I tried to ignore the comment but she wouldn't let up.

"We've tried so hard to move on from those days, Paige. This is going to call into question everything we've worked for. Everything your father worked so hard to accomplish. You've taken that from him."

"I didn't take anything from him. This has no reflection on the two of you."

"If this doesn't reflect on us as parents, who does it reflect on?"

"Me. I was the one who made the poor decision. And I've paid the price. I'm done keeping secrets. This was so difficult to reveal, but I feel a strange sense of freedom."

"Other people have to bear the burden of your freedom. It's one thing if you had told this girl when you were alone, somewhere private where she could process the news and not become a spectacle. You've done irreparable harm."

My stomach clenched. But I wasn't about to admit that I feared she was right. "Mom, thank you, but I'll wait to see what kind of response we get from Treha. And she's not 'this girl,' she's your granddaughter."

"I know perfectly well who she is."

My phone buzzed and I looked at the call waiting, which said simply *Treha.*

"Can you hang on, Mom? I have another call."

"I'm sure it's much more important."

I hit the button. "Treha? I was just talking about you with my mother. How are you?"

"I'm fine."

Her voice had already become familiar. The short, clipped words. I imagined her looking at the ground as she spoke.

"Good. I hope we can get together later today. Would you be up for dinner?"

"Actually I was calling about the picture."

"Yes, I have it right here, along with some other pictures I thought you might like to see."

"Can you bring them? This morning?"

"Well, I'm on my way to school at the moment."

"It's important."

Treha's tone sounded a little strained, and the last thing I wanted to do was let her down at this point, even if it made me late. "I'll be right there. Can you meet me outside in the parking lot?"

"Yes."

"All right. Be there in about twenty minutes. See you then. Oh, Treha — have you talked with your friends in Arizona yet?"

The phone clicked. I listened to the silence, then returned to my mother's line. There was noise in the background, some disturbance.

"Mom?"

It took a few seconds but she came back on the line. "Paige, are you there?"

"Yes, that was Treha."

"I need to go. Your father is having an episode."

"Is it serious?"

"He's just agitated. Go on with your life and don't worry about us."

She hung up as my father yelled in the background.

I found Treha just inside the entrance gate to Bethesda, waiting, her hair tousled by the wind and falling leaves encircling her. She wore jeans and a scrub top and stood with her arms folded.

My daughter. She wasn't just a concept any longer or a secret to hide from my friends. She was flesh and blood and bone and heart.

I pulled to the curb and retrieved the pictures and got out.

"How are you this morning?" I said, giving her a slight hug.

"Fine." No emotion. No return hug.

"I was going to ask you if you'd spoken with any of your friends back in Arizona yet. Miriam or Elsie?"

She looked at the ground. "Not yet."

"Well, that's going to be a fun phone call, don't you think?" My voice was too bright. Trying too hard.

Treha didn't respond.

"Have you spoken with anyone about what happened last night?"

"Just Anna."

"Anna? Do I know her?"

"I don't think so."

"Well, evidently our reunion has stirred some reaction. Someone took a video —"

"Anna showed it to me. Did you bring the picture?"

"Yes. I actually have several. Now these are originals, so take care of them."

As soon as I said it, I regretted it. I sounded like a controlling mother, a worrywart. I sounded like my own mother. Treha had every right to rip the photos up in front of me and toss them to the wind or make a collage or do whatever she wanted.

"I'll make sure you get them back."

"Of course you will. I just meant these are . . . Well, they can't be replaced."

"Is this him?"

"Yes. You have the same facial features, don't you think?"

She stared at the photo as if it might come alive if she concentrated hard enough. "And this is you."

"Younger, happier. Not a care in the world. I had no idea what would happen in such a short time. But this is behind us now, isn't it? This is the past we're holding." I flipped to another picture. "These are your grandparents. I have a couple of other pictures in there of me when I was pregnant with you. Not a soul on the planet has seen those, Treha."

She kept staring as if they were a puzzle to decipher. Finally she looked at me and said, "Thank you."

I rushed on, encouraged by the eye contact. "I was thinking we could pick up something for dinner and you could come to my house tonight. Would that be okay?"

"I guess so."

"Do you like Chinese? Pizza? Whatever you want."

"Chinese is fine."

"Great. I'll bring a menu and we can order on the way. I'll pick you up here around five thirty?"

"Okay."

Treha turned and walked back toward the school and I gave a huge sigh. This was going to be harder than it looked. Probably a lot harder. But there are things worth doing once you commit to them, and motherhood is one of them. I had gotten over the hurdle of unveiling. Now I had to get over the hurdle of Treha's heart.

CHAPTER 27

Treha

Treha's migraine was a beast. Pressure on both of her temples and squiggly lines scrolling across her field of vision. Closing her eyes didn't help — it actually made things worse. It was like stepping into a minefield and watching the shrapnel fly, even though she wasn't moving.

She stayed in her room with the lights off and didn't go to class. She couldn't. Couldn't bear the stares or questions that might come from well-meaning students who wanted to ask how she felt about finding her mother.

Anna found her in the room later that morning. She picked up the picture of Treha's father. "He's pretty cute."

"He's dead."

"Okay, he *was* pretty cute. Sorry."

"Take care of the picture — that's the only copy she has."

"All right, Treha. Thanks for trusting me."

Anna left and a few moments later Treha's cell phone buzzed. She hoped it wasn't her mother. The buzz was like a percussive bomb going off, even though it was just vibrating. The questions running through her pounding head were almost as bad as the noise.

Instead of her mother, it was Miriam from Tucson.

"Treha, I heard there's something going on between you and your roommate. How are you doing?"

There's a lot going on with everyone, Treha thought. "She accused me of stealing."

"Is there any truth to it?" Miriam said.

"No."

"Of course not."

"I've never seen her jewelry. Why would I want it? Why would I steal it?"

"I'm sorry you're having to go through this. I keep kicking myself for not saying something the first day I was there. I knew this would be a problem."

"How did you find out?"

"Your RA called. Jill thought I should contact you."

Treha listened to the woman's voice. It was nice to hear someone she trusted, someone who had her best interests at heart.

"Treha," Miriam said slowly, as if she were even more concerned about what she was about to say. "Jill also mentioned what happened last night. The video someone took."

"Oh."

"She said everyone there knows about it. That it's online."

Treha didn't respond. The pain in her head was overpowering, and now her stomach clenched.

"Do you think it's true?"

"Yes. Ms. Redwine told me she wrote the letter."

A pause. "How do you feel, Treha? You've waited your whole life to find her, and to think she was right there . . ."

"She waited a long time to tell me," Treha said. "I think she was scared what would happen."

"Did you have a good talk with her?"

"It was okay."

"You sound discouraged," Miriam said.

"I have a migraine."

"I'm sorry. I know how debilitating those can be. Get some rest and shut the phone off, okay?"

Treha paused, the longing in her heart leaking through the phone line.

"Treha, there's no pressure for you to feel

a certain way or to feel something you don't."

"It's been my one dream . . . My mother wants to have dinner with me and I'm in my room . . ."

"Okay, so you're in your room. You're having a hard time with the news. This is okay. You're feeling something. That's good. Listen to it. Respond to it."

"I'm feeling like I want to come home."

A slight pause on the other end. "Really, Treha?"

"I don't know. I'm just scared of what's happening."

"Well, you're free to come back here at any point. You know that. You have your own credit card. You can make a reservation and come home during Thanksgiving break or this weekend if you want. If you need to tell your mother that you want some time to think about all this, do that. If you need to be alone, she'll understand. She's probably going through a lot of emotions herself. And if you want to come here and decompress, do it."

"But you don't think I should."

"This is not about what you should or shouldn't do. This is about you, okay?" Miriam paused to hear some response on the phone. When Treha didn't give one, she sighed. "Elsie and I will have an all-day prayer meeting on your behalf. Charlie might even fast from his oatmeal, so you know how important this is. And I know that you're going to make a good decision. Okay? Get some rest. See if you can overcome the migraine. Things will be a lot clearer when you get past this."

Treha thanked her and hung up. The sun shone brightly through the cracks in the crooked blinds. Treha put a pillow over her head and tried to go back to sleep.

CHAPTER 28

Paige

Dr. Waldron stepped into my office shortly after I arrived that morning, as I was trying desperately to focus on preparations for my first class.

"Paige, we need to talk." He sat down, letting me know this was not a conversation for later, not optional.

"Certainly," I said, glancing at the clock on the wall.

He scratched at the top of his balding head. "The news about what happened at Bethesda last night is running up and down the corridors. It has us concerned."

I bristled immediately. "My private life has no bearing —"

"The public nature of this is what I'm talking about. You revealed yourself to this girl in a common area, with other students in earshot."

"I didn't know . . ." I took a breath. "I

agree the choice of location wasn't the wisest. It never occurred to me that others might be listening. I would've never exposed Treha like that. But I don't see why you're concerned."

He gave me the look of an exasperated parent whose child should know better. "Paige, you teach at Bethesda as a representative of Millhaven. Your actions are a reflection on this school as well as —"

"I can't imagine the mental gymnastics someone would have to go through in order to take my teaching at Bethesda as a negative. I'm teaching them how to write, how to read great literature and understand it."

"Have you thought of the irony there? That you're teaching young people to write when you can't?"

I sighed. "I pride myself on being a living, breathing example of irony, Dr. Waldron. Now if you'll excuse me, I still have classes to teach."

I gathered my things to head out the door but the man didn't move. "Paige, wait."

Everything inside me clenched, but I forced myself to pause, to lower my shoulders and hear him out.

"Perhaps I was unwise to give my okay for the class at Bethesda. I thought it might be good for you. I thought this might help you get on track with your thesis. Now I'm questioning my judgment."

"What's to question?" I said. "If this is about my thesis, I'm going to get it done. I feel closer than ever. Seriously, this whole thing with my daughter has freed me up in a way that I could never have imagined. . . ."

"Are you sure about this young woman? That she's your daughter?"

"I'm positive."

"And . . . did you know about her when you agreed to teach at Bethesda? Did you know she was assigned to your class?"

"No . . ." I hesitated. "Well, I learned she would be in my class just before it began. But I'd had no idea she would be at Bethesda. I considered having her removed from my class or removing myself, but . . ." How could I explain my indecision or the whole series of choices and nonchoices that had led us here? I shrugged helplessly and let him do what he would with that.

Dr. Waldron studied me for a long moment, then nodded. "It's a lot to take in. And coming on the heels of the situation with your parents . . . I wonder if you might need some time to process all of this. Time away."

I stared at him in disbelief and put my laptop case on the desk. When I had collected myself, I said, "I'm fine. I don't need time away."

"Paige, no one here is against you. This is a storm we need to face together. I want to help us navigate the ship to the other side."

I resisted the urge to call him *captain.* "I appreciate that, but I assure you, there's nothing keeping me from doing my job. Now I really need to get to my class."

"All right. Let's talk again this afternoon."

I walked quickly, feeling an overwhelming sense of dread. Fortunately I had a deep novel to discuss in my first class, and after a while I lost myself in the rhythm of teaching. The students didn't know it, but they helped me get through the day.

After my last class of the afternoon, I checked my phone and saw that Treha had texted.

Something has come up. I can't go with you to dinner.

I stopped in the hallway, wondering what could have happened. Perhaps she was having second thoughts about me as a mother. I went over our conversation at the IHOP. Maybe she thought I was cheap. I would have taken her to a much nicer place but I thought she would like the casual setting. It would help her feel less nervous, more relaxed.

Becoming aware of students passing beside and around me, I ducked into the elevator and typed, That's fine, Treha. Can't wait to see you.

I deleted that and started over again. No problem, Treha. Call me when . . . I backspaced. I didn't want to give Treha any double message or suggestion that she had to take care of me. She had to feel my strength throughout this honeymoon period, if there was such a thing. The relationship had to come slowly, at her pace. As much or as little as she wanted.

No problem, Treha. I love you.

There. That was it. I pushed the Send button and looked up. A female student I'd never seen stared at me.

"You're Ms. Redwine, aren't you?"

"Yes."

"I saw your video. That was amazing."

"Thank you," I said.

"What was the video?" someone beside her asked.

The doors opened and even though it wasn't my floor, I exited as the student began describing what she had seen. I took the stairs to my office and checked the other messages. There was one from a local news station. How do these people get personal phone numbers? Two women from my reading group. I wondered if Beverly had heard the news and how high she jumped when she discovered that Treha finally knew me as her mother and not just as her teacher.

As strong as I wanted to be, as much as I wanted to absorb any pain, the text from Treha concerned me. I didn't want to overreact but I was counting on being with her, getting to know her, and her getting to know me. As soon as I got to the office, I closed the door and dialed my mother. There was no answer, which didn't make sense. Mom was always there. She had people from her church retrieve groceries. Perhaps there was an emergency or just a doctor's appointment.

"Mom, it's Paige. Can you call me?"

I sat at my desk, staring at the unopened mail, the ungraded papers, equally paralyzed by the past and the future. I looked at Treha's text again to see if I had missed something in the first reading. Can you tell tone by a text? Can you tell heartache or a cry for help?

A knock at the door. I stayed seated, paralyzed. Thankfully, I had pictures of great writers plastered over the window so no one could see inside.

"Do you know if Ms. Redwine is in?" I heard Dr. Waldron say.

"She's usually here at this time, but I didn't see her return from class."

I kept silent. The department secretary had been out when I came in. I could have just stood and opened the door, but I was glued to the chair. I could exit the window, but I didn't have any bedsheets to tie together.

"I'll come back," Dr. Waldron said. "Would you call me when she returns?"

"Yes, Dr. Waldron."

I looked out the window and watched the sun run its successive journey. The office phone rang and I didn't move. The secretary answered and I heard her say I hadn't returned. A little part of me jumped inside, happy to be hidden.

I went to the door and peeled back a corner of Flannery O'Connor's face to see the outer office, watching until the secretary went to the restroom. It was then that I gathered my things and quietly closed the office door behind me and slipped to the stairwell. I took the back exit off campus, the one without the security guard at the shack, and was on my way.

I had been looking forward to Chinese and conversation with Treha, asking her questions this time, and part of me wanted to make it happen. I debated finding her in the commons but decided that was too forward. So I sat in Bethesda's parking lot and watched from a distance, my cell phone going crazy with calls and texts. None of them were from Treha, no matter how much I wanted to hear that her schedule was now free and she wanted to meet.

I searched through the messages again and wrote Treha a text, then deleted it. It was hard to go back after getting a taste of what it might be like to be a real mother, to show real love in tangible ways. But love is a two-way street. I knew that. God does not force himself on us. We must be receptive. And so it was with Treha.

I thought I saw her walking toward the commons, her backpack slapping up and down, her hair bouncing. I even got out of the car and willed her to turn, but when she did, I saw another face, another student.

Finally I couldn't take it any longer. I pulled up her number and the call went straight to voice mail. I hung up quickly, wondering what had happened. Maybe she'd gone on a date, a real date with a boy. She had asked what the first kiss was like and I imagined her as shy and inexperienced, sitting on the periphery of life.

I dialed again and this time let the message play, listening to the recorded phone voice and then to my daughter's voice saying her name, Treha Langsam. The vowels were swallowed and there was a certain breathy quality.

"Treha, I thought I would call one more time and make sure you hadn't changed your mind. Even if you are out late, I can still come by and pick you up if you want. But it's whatever you want. No pressure. I just want you to know I'm here and open and ready for another talk. Okay, hope you're having a good evening."

I hung up and felt defeated, felt like I had just done irreparable harm to the relationship. For all I knew, Treha never wanted to see me again.

I wasn't hungry, at least not for food, so I sat there. I dialed my mother but got her answering machine again.

Then the phone buzzed in my hand and I nearly dropped it. The name on the screen said *Treha*. I answered and heard background noise, people talking, something said loudly behind her, like in a cafeteria. Treha's voice was muffled.

"I'm sorry. I didn't get that, Treha. What did you say?"

"I heard your message. I can't have dinner with you. I don't want to."

"Treha, why? What's wrong?"

"Anna found out the truth. I left the pictures with her at Bethesda. She said she would send them to you. I didn't lose them."

"Treha, back up. I don't understand."

"I don't know why you lied to me."

"Lied?"

"It doesn't matter now. I can't do this."

"What did I lie about?"

The call cut off. My heart fluttered, beat a hundred miles an hour, and I felt disoriented, like the world had turned upside down and was spinning. What could she be talking about?

I made my way into the Bethesda cafeteria, searching the rows of tables. As I continued, students noticed, pointing at me. I must have looked out of place as a professor where professors dared not go. Or maybe they recognized me from the video.

"Ms. Redwine!" A female student from my writing class waved from the corner and came forward. "What are you doing here?"

"I'm looking for Treha. Have you seen her?"

She shook her head and looked around. "No. She usually sits back there."

"She mentioned a friend of hers. Anna? Do you know her?"

"Sure, Anna Waddel. I think I saw her . . . Yeah, there she is. Blue top at the table right behind the pillar."

"Thank you." I said it absently, hoping that Treha would somehow be at the table and willing to talk. Anna was sitting alone, however, and her eyes grew wide when she saw me approach.

"I have something for you, Ms. Redwine," Anna said. She pulled out an envelope and handed it to me. "I was going to mail it to you. Treha said you needed them back."

I stuffed the envelope in my purse. "Where is she?"

The girl looked sheepishly at her salad, then back up. "She said she was going to call you. Tell you what we found. I didn't mean for it to turn out this way. Honestly, I didn't."

"Turn out what way?"

"She didn't call you?"

"She said I lied to her. What was she talking about? Does she think I'm not her mother?"

Anna frowned. "I told her I wouldn't talk about this. Or write about it. I'm not even supposed to tell you where she's —"

"You're not supposed to tell me what? Anna, where is my daughter?"

Something inside took over and I grabbed the girl by an arm as if I could wrench the truth from her. I'm not a violent person, but I wasn't going to let go until she told me. "Where did she go?"

"She left, Ms. Redwine."

I loosened my grip and searched the girl's eyes.

"She got Cameron to give her a ride. A friend of hers."

"A ride where?"

"To the airport. She said she was going home. To Arizona."

The background noise. It wasn't from a cafeteria. It was the airport. I ran from the room to the parking lot and got in my car.

I drove toward the airport, calling her number again and again, but by the time I drew close, I knew. Treha was gone and wasn't coming back.

Chapter 29

Treha

Treha awoke the next morning at first light. The brewing coffee was the first thing she noticed, the smell wafting through the house like the perfume of a welcome friend. She sat up in bed in the spare room of Miriam and Charlie Howard and looked out the window at the Catalina Mountains. There were fewer trees here and very little grass, but the view was magnificent. There had been a chill in the air back in Tennessee, but there was not even a hint of it here.

Her migraine was gone. So was the feeling that she was living in the wrong place with the wrong people, cooped up in a dorm full of young women who didn't understand. She didn't belong at Bethesda. She didn't belong with those smart professors and good-looking students who wore nice clothes and had answers to all the questions.

She was back in her old outfit of scrubs,

and the familiar clothing gave her a peaceful feeling. It felt like belonging. She walked into the hall and saw movement in the kitchen but turned left and headed to Charlie's office. She had missed the man. He wasn't the most talkative person on the planet, but that felt good. There was a quiet confidence to his silence.

Charlie was behind his computer watching the early morning stocks from overseas tick by on the screen. A television was on across the room, mounted to the wall, tuned to Bloomberg. The local talk radio station was on in the background but somewhat muted, a commercial promoting a website to watch a video about a talking dog.

"How'd you sleep?" he said, not looking up from the screen. Some people would feel it awkward to talk with someone like Charlie but Treha found it easier than having someone look at her and expect her to respond.

"Okay. It felt good to be back in my old bed again."

"I'll bet. Those dorm room mattresses can be a real pain."

She sat in a chair near his desk and stared at the constant movement on the screen.

"I've got a stack of crossword puzzles I haven't been able to finish. Just waiting for you to come back and help me."

Treha hadn't said much to Miriam on the way home from the airport. The woman had asked if she wanted to go to Desert Gardens with her today and Treha said she would sleep on it. Part of her wanted to stay in bed all day. Another part of her wanted to sit with Elsie and listen to her and talk. Part of her didn't want to talk about any of it.

Charlie turned and took off his glasses. "I have to say, selfishly, I'm glad you're back. Miriam hasn't been the same with you gone. She picks up the phone about a hundred times every night and kind of rubs it like you're the genie in a bottle, hoping you'll materialize. You not being here has increased her prayer life. That's one positive."

"Is it okay with you if I stay here?"

"Fine with me. I want what's best. We both do."

"And what do you think is best?"

He looked back at the screen. "Today, with oil futures rising, the best is probably going to be one of the big companies. Maybe Exxon Mobil."

"I'm not talking about stocks."

"I know you're not, but you're also not really looking for advice. I don't have any idea what the best thing is for you, Treha.

I've never been a parent. But I have a sense that you're going to figure it out. And the best thing we can do is just be here to watch you take the ride."

Treha had never heard Charlie speak so many words. "Did you hear that my mother found me?"

"My ear is still ringing from the whoop that Miriam let out. Nearly gave me a heart attack."

"She's not who I thought she would be."

Charlie nodded and looked at the screen again. "Not many of us are."

"Why do people lie?"

"Probably because they're scared of the truth. I think deep down we're trying to figure things out. Find where we belong. Some of us come to rest in a ditch and it's too hard to get out, so we get stuck and pretty soon stuck becomes comfortable and we just stay there. While others do the hard thing."

"Where are you?" Treha said. "Are you doing the hard thing or are you stuck?"

"I moved the furniture into the ditch." He smiled and looked at her from the corner of his eye. "You should get something to eat. Want me to make you something?"

Treha shook her head. She sat a few minutes listening to the conversation on the radio, the mixed voices of reporters on TV talking about the latest financial news, and the voices inside her head asking the questions that were too hard to answer.

CHAPTER 30

Paige

I dodged Dr. Waldron as long as I could, but the man and the consequences finally caught up with me on Wednesday. I was strongly encouraged to take a leave of absence. Saying no was not an option, especially after the scene I'd made in the Bethesda cafeteria the night before. When I asked Dr. Waldron how long a leave he was recommending, he would only say, "Let's see how things go, shall we?"

I suppose I went into shock that afternoon as I packed up essential books and memorabilia from my office. I went home and drifted through the next two days. Thinking about Treha, thinking about my job, and trying not to think about either.

Perhaps my mother had been right all along. Keeping these things submerged was better. Revelation only brings pain and spills on everyone else like waves of toxic chemicals. I'd had the perfect opportunity to let my daughter go, to stay hidden and let her find her way in the world. But that chance had slipped through my fingers the moment I decided to engage with her and reveal myself. If I had stayed hidden, life would have been much simpler, much less complicated for everyone. And I would still be in her life, still speaking to her, reading her words, listening to her and walking alongside as her teacher.

Friday evening was the next meeting of the reading group, this time at Beverly's home. I had hoped I could bring Treha but that wasn't to be. I didn't want to attend. I wanted to crawl into bed and never get out again. Maybe fall through a rabbit hole and stay there with Alice and her friends. But something told me I needed this, that I needed to push through the disappointment and shock and be with people who cared.

The women of the group gathered with wineglasses in hand and surrounded me with their love and understanding. Like Job's friends they sat in silence for a while, the sound of the fire crackling in Beverly's living room. It felt uncomfortable at first and I wanted to fill the void with words or laughter or explanation or description. But sometimes the void is better left open.

"I think you're on the right track, Paige," Ginny Baylor said. "With your daughter. With taking some time away from school. This is going to leave you better off in the long run."

"What you let go will come back to you if you love well," Madalyn said. It sounded like something on a greeting card you buy for $1.99 in the discontinued card section of the grocery store.

"How long have you known?" Esther Richards said. "About your daughter, that she was out there?"

"I've known where she is for more than a year."

"You did everything you could to help her."

Encouragement. Support. They wanted me to know I was loved, that I was not alone, and everything about it felt assuring and lovely except for the look on Beverly's face. There was something going on there I couldn't decipher.

Finally I said, "I don't want to bring the meeting down. This doesn't have to be about me. In fact, I think it would be best to do what we usually do. That probably would help more than anything."

"And what is it we do here, Paige?" Beverly said. Her voice was sharp, edgy.

"We share the things we love about literature," I said, mildly bewildered by the question. "This is about the stories."

"No, that's not really it, is it?" She looked around at the others and they grunted and nodded. "It's not really about the stories. It's never been just about that."

"What do you mean?"

She leaned closer without smiling. The others were silent, staring at the fire. Either praying or waiting their turn to pile on or disagree.

"We've been meeting together for years," Beverly continued. "We've gone through cancer, a divorce, a couple of major surgeries. Family members dying. Pets. Abandonment. Betrayal. Job losses. Through all of that we have grown together. We've said that there is nothing we can't share with each other. Am I right?"

I nodded, studying the way the firelight reflected off the dull hardwood.

"We have shared things here we haven't shared with any other human on the planet. And you have been walking around with this wound, a gaping hole, a weight you have carried alone."

"I'm sorry. I should have told you sooner." I looked up at their faces and the stares back at me weren't hard or judgmental but from soft eyes. Still, I took umbrage. "I didn't expect to be jumped on."

"I'm not doing that, Paige. This is a pivotal moment for you, for all of us. What happened with your daughter is one of those deep wounds. What the school did to you might not have been fair. But there's something more to this. Something much bigger."

"Well, if you figure it out, please tell me. I've been asking God for a long time why all this is happening."

"Beverly, what she needs right now is not our advice," Madalyn said. "She needs our love."

"Yes, she needs our love," Beverly said. "But love sometimes looks like a kick in the pants."

I wanted to get up and leave, to simply walk out, hurt and abandoned by the people who were *for* me. But I stayed for some reason, and the words came. "How much of the past do I have to deal with? Do I have to dredge up everything and parade it in front of everyone?"

"Those are two different questions. But the first is the most important. Let me ask this, Paige. How much of your past do you want God to redeem?" Beverly wouldn't let me out of her sight. "How much of your regret and sorrow do you want him to forgive and use? For your good and his glory? You want to give him all of it, right?"

I nodded weakly.

"Life doesn't come from stuffing it in the closet or holding it under the water. Come out of the shadows. Take a breath. See what freedom tastes like, smells like, feels like. It's *time.*"

I closed my eyes. From my pocket, I dug out my father's pen, the one he made, the talisman of my life that on some level still worked, still gave comfort.

Finally Beverly spoke again. "You're a mother, Paige. What do you intend to do about your daughter?"

"I don't know."

She cocked her head and I realized my infraction.

"Okay, let me just . . . think," I said, holding up a hand. I tapped the pen against my leg. "The honest truth is, my plan right now is to let her decide. To let her go and let her see if she wants to keep the distance between us or decide that she wants a relationship. Isn't that what God does with us? Doesn't he allow us the choice of whether to respond to him or not?"

"He does, but that's usually after a fair amount of pursuing by the Hound of

Heaven."

"So you think I should go after her."

"I think the familiar misery is easier to live with than what might happen if you pursue her."

Esther cleared her throat. "Beverly, I think you're being too hard on her."

"Am I?"

"Treha doesn't want a relationship with me," I said. "She flew to Arizona to get away from me."

"She's testing you. She's calling you out instead of letting you relate to her on your own terms."

"I don't think she believes I'm her mother."

"Tough. You are. She'll get over that."

"She said I lied to her. She can't deal with being lied to."

"What did she mean?"

"I'm not sure. I'm assuming she —"

"You're assuming? Paige, the time for assuming is over. Go to her. Talk with her. Find out what's going on in her mind. You are her mother. Act like it."

I looked at my mentor, my friend, the woman who had saved my life. How could I not trust her, not believe she was right?

Ginny bent forward. "I think you should go to her, Paige. Take the chance to be rejected. Get this out in the open. And we'll be praying for you and cheering you on."

Chapter 31

Treha

Treha hung around the house with Charlie a few days but finally rode with Miriam to Desert Gardens Retirement Home on Saturday morning. She walked through the hallways in her scrubs and the memories flooded back. Dr. Crenshaw's room had been taken by another man, something that made her sad because she had sat with him evening after evening going through word games. She was pleasantly surprised that Mrs. Williams was doing so well. During the time Treha worked at Desert Gardens, the woman had fallen from her bed and broken her hip. She looked alert and was glad to see Treha.

Treha walked the grounds with Buck Davis, the aged security guard who had been at the facility as long as Miriam had. He asked about her time away at school, oblivious to the problems she had encountered, but she didn't mind the questions. She knew he just cared.

She held off meeting with Elsie until lunch. The woman hugged her tightly when they met at the windowed side of the cafeteria, the side most avoided. A staff member served them like they were royalty.

Elsie took Treha's hand when she sat and wouldn't let go, cradling it with arthritic fingers. "I prayed for you every minute I was awake, my girl. I'm so glad to see you."

Treha stared at the food, which looked a lot like the food at Bethesda. She pushed the tray back and prepared for the inevitable questions. But when questions come from someone you love, you don't mind.

"Tell me what you thought of the school."

"It was nice. I liked the rooms and the buildings. How clean it was."

"What about the people? The professors?"

"I learned a lot. The teachers were kind. I think they want people to learn as much as they can."

"Miriam said you had trouble with a roommate. Don't judge the place on one bad apple."

"I didn't."

"But if you're back here, you must be thinking of quitting."

"I don't think it's the best place for me."

"Because of this English teacher who says she's your mother?"

Treha nodded.

"Miriam told me about that. At least as much as she knows. I tried to see it on the computer but I don't know how those things work. My nephew brought his little contraption over and he found the video. She seemed genuine, didn't she? You're a good judge of that."

"I thought she was. But I found out that she didn't tell me the truth about something, and when a person doesn't tell the truth about one thing, can you believe anything she says?"

"I see your point. That does tend to make you skittish. Well, I suppose you can just take a blood test and settle the whole thing, can't you?"

"Even if she is my mother, I don't know that I would want to have a relationship with her."

"Must be a whopper of a lie." Elsie waved a hand. "It's none of my business, of course. But how did you find out about this mysterious lie she told?"

"I have a friend, Anna. She's the one who found out about the lie."

"I see. So you did make a friend."

Treha nodded.

Elsie spooned some soup into her mouth, then crushed a small package of saltines and tried to open it. Treha opened the wrapper and sprinkled the crackers on her soup the way Elsie liked it.

"Thank you, my dear. You don't know how many times I've wanted those and I just haven't been able to get that package open." She stirred her spoon around the bowl. "Kind of like life, in a way. What you want is right there, so close you can taste it. Sometimes you need somebody else to open it."

Treha picked at her food.

"What do you think you want to do about all of this?" Elsie finally said. "Do you have a plan?"

"I don't want to let you down. You helped pay for my schooling."

"Don't let money make the decision. You decide what's best, what you want to do. That money was an investment in you. Period. Do you understand?"

"Thank you."

"So you have a choice, and it's not about money. What do you want to do?"

Treha looked around the dining room at the tables, the older people talking and laughing. Some were alone, locked away. Others were vibrant and connected, like

Elsie. "Part of me wants to come back here. To work with Miriam and you."

"And we'd love to have you. You know that." Elsie took a deep breath. "But deep down that feels like giving up, doesn't it?"

Treha looked at her, searching the old woman's eyes.

"The natural thing for an old geezer like me is to want things to stay the same. Want things to stop changing. Keep things the way they are or go back to the way they've been. I think that's why we get cranky in our old age. The world passes, leaves us sitting at the stoplight. You were built for more than this place, Treha. I can feel that."

Treha put down her fork and took a sip of water.

Elsie reached out a hand and took Treha's. "The Lord knows your heart. He knows your hopes, dreams. He knows what's best." She closed her eyes tightly and began to pray. "Lord, you know Treha's heart's desire. We don't understand all that's happened. We don't know how it all fits together. But we trust you, not just in what we can understand, but in what we don't. And we want your will. Show her the next step. Make her heart's desire what you desire."

Elsie squeezed Treha's hand, and when

Treha looked up, Miriam was standing next to the table, a concerned look on her face.

"Treha, I'm sorry to interrupt. There's someone here who would like to see you."

Treha glanced behind Miriam and saw someone standing at the back entrance who took her breath away.

"Who is it, Treha?" Elsie said.

"Ms. Redwine. My teacher. My mother."

Ms. Redwine walked gingerly to the table and smiled at Treha and Elsie. Treha stared at her, not believing she was there. She searched for air, a breath, what to say.

Elsie put down her napkin. "You've got a lot of nerve coming in here, sister."

"I apologize. I know I shouldn't have come without an invitation."

"Her mother would have come a long time ago." Elsie raised her voice and Miriam stood behind the older woman, her hands on her shoulders, calming her a little.

Ms. Redwine knelt on the floor in front of Treha. "When you left, a thousand thoughts flew through my mind. I knew I had to make a choice. Last night something happened. I realized so much of this has been about how afraid I've been." She looked at Elsie and Miriam. "I wish I'd come here sooner. I would choose differently if I had it to do over. I can only hope that as you hear the story, you'll understand and forgive me."

Miriam pulled a chair around and Ms. Redwine sat. Treha kept her distance from the woman and stared at the table.

"I've heard about you from Treha," Ms. Redwine said. "And I actually saw the film some time ago, when it was in theaters."

"You saw your daughter in a movie and you didn't come see her?" Elsie said. She shook her head. "I don't understand people. Is this what they teach professors in school these days? Because if it is, I don't want Treha to have anything to do with them."

"What I meant to say was, thank you for being there for her when I couldn't be."

"Couldn't or didn't want to?" Elsie said.

People stared at the stranger in their midst. Those who knew Treha looked concerned at the scene unfolding.

"Maybe we should take this conversation to my office," Miriam said.

"Maybe we should take this woman to the woodshed," Elsie muttered. She looked up again, spiking her napkin into her soup and wagging a finger. "Do you have any idea what this girl has been through? Do you have any idea the pain she felt not knowing where she came from? And you come waltzing in here dressed in your jeans and carrying your expensive purse and expect us all to fall down and give a thank offering. Somebody said you graduated from Bethesda?"

"That's right."

"Well, if this is the kind of people they're putting out these days, I'm glad Treha's not going there, missy."

Ms. Redwine was near tears now and Miriam found a napkin and handed it to her.

"I understand your anger. You have every right. And it shows you really care about my daughter. I have so many regrets."

Treha's fingers began to type on the table in front of her. She felt her eye movement kick in and she began to sway forward and backward in her chair. They were talking about her as if she weren't in the room.

"Well, it took you an awfully long time to do anything about it."

"Maybe it *would* be better if we talked in private," Ms. Redwine said.

"Excuse me," Treha said. In one motion she pushed away from the table and ran toward the hallway.

Chapter 32

Paige

The journey of a thousand miles begins with a credit card. I'd taken the earliest flight possible, and because of the time difference, I was on the ground in Tucson with my carry-on luggage by 10:45 a.m. Navigating my way from the airport to Desert Gardens was surprisingly easy, but walking into that facility was one of the most difficult things I've ever done.

Elsie was an elderly hurdle all her own. Her back was up from the moment we met. I'd known that the people who cared for Treha would feel like this. And strangely, I wouldn't have wanted it any other way. I wanted people to defend Treha, take her side, show loyalty and concern. Inside, I was grateful to God for sheltering her.

What I hadn't planned was Treha running from the dining hall and out of the facility. Miriam stopped me from following and suggested we give her some time. She asked the security guard, Buck, to make sure Treha was okay. The two had a special relationship, evidently. Meanwhile Miriam, Elsie, and I moved to Miriam's office. We made small talk as we waited but that quickly turned into a series of questions about my life. Elsie wanted to know when I had studied at Bethesda, how I came to teach at Millhaven, when I decided to come to Arizona, and how much I paid for the ticket on such short notice.

"I decided last night after some friends helped me see what's at stake," I said, dodging her question about the ticket cost.

"And what is that?" Miriam said.

"The heart of my daughter. She's more important than anything."

Elsie frowned. "Why did it take so long to realize that?"

"She's always been on my mind. I've thought of her every day."

"Listen, sister, thinking about someone and doing something about it are two wildly different things. I get the same kind of letters from family members who never visit. 'We're thinking of you.' 'We hope to see you soon.' That kind of thing. Doesn't mean a hoot if you don't show up. And the truth is, you didn't show up for more than twenty years."

Elsie and Beverly would make good friends. "I don't have a good answer for that. Except I thought I was loving Treha. I thought she was in a good family situation and I didn't want to disrupt that."

"But you saw the film," Miriam said before Elsie could launch in again. "You knew Treha wanted to find you. And you still waited. When she showed up in your class, even then you kept the truth hidden."

"Yes." I sighed. "This is part of what I realized last night. How much I've been guided by my fear. All my life."

"So why have you come now?" Elsie said with a new level of tenacity. "You've gotten over your fear and you took an early flight, but what's the purpose? What do you intend to do?"

I took a deep breath. "I'm going to do whatever it takes to show my daughter I'm ready to be her mother."

Elsie raised her eyebrows but said nothing.

"For some reason she thinks I'm lying. I'm not. I've been truthful the entire time."

"Every minute you taught that girl and didn't tell her you were her mother, every essay or test you graded and didn't reveal yourself, you were lying," Elsie said.

I wanted to argue, wanted to defend myself, but I swallowed that. "I see your point. I understand why you would feel that way, but I haven't lied to her."

"We'll have to disagree about that," Elsie said.

"What is it she thinks I'm lying about? If it's me being her mother, that can be cleared up with a simple test."

"I don't have any idea," Elsie said. "I had only begun to talk with her when you blew in on an east wind."

I looked at Miriam.

"I think that ought to come from Treha," Miriam said. "But I hope you can tell we're her staunch supporters. We'll do anything we can to see that she's not hurt again."

"I understand it was you two who helped her with the funds to come to Bethesda in the first place."

The two looked at each other and Elsie took over. "We would do anything for that girl. Anything at all. There's been no one to take up her case, no one to fight for her. To see her hurt further is unconscionable."

They kept questioning me from there. They wanted to know about Dr. Crenshaw. They wanted to know about the depression medication and other things uncovered through the documentary. Then came questions about Treha's conception and her father and before long I was sharing details I hadn't shared even with my own mother. I wanted to show them my life was an open book. In truth, I wanted them to like me, to encourage Treha to come to my side. But my job was to reach Treha. If her friends warmed to me, in the end, that was icing on the cake.

"So what do you propose?" Elsie said finally. "What are you going to do with our girl? You going to try to take her back to Bethesda? Do you want her to live with you?"

Another deep breath. "I actually haven't gotten that far. Bottom line, I want whatever is best for Treha. If she wants to come live with me, my home is open. If she wants to go to Bethesda, I'll help make that happen. If you want to be reimbursed for her school fees —"

"You can forget about that," Elsie said. "The money we gave was an investment in that girl's life. You're not taking that away from us."

"I appreciate everything you've done. I'm not trying to take anything away, and honestly, if Treha said she wanted to stay here and work with you, Miriam, I would support that." I gritted my teeth and swallowed hard. The words came easier than the feeling. "This is about Treha. This is not about what I need."

Miriam stood as the door to the office opened.

One of the facility's female workers poked her head in. "Mrs. Howard, Buck called. He tried to follow Treha on foot but she ran too fast. He's in the car now, but he hasn't been able to find her. He was wondering if you would like to help."

Miriam looked at me and I grabbed my purse. Elsie grabbed her walker like she was going as well.

"Maybe you should stay here and pray," Miriam told her.

"I can pray in the backseat just as easy as I can here." In the car, I dialed Treha's number but there was no answer. Miriam called and left a message saying we just wanted to know she was all right. As we drove, Miriam pointed out different places that were important to Treha.

"Could she have gone back to your house?"

"It's too far to walk. I think she's probably near here — that's the coffee shop where her bike was once stolen."

"What about her old apartment?" I said.

Miriam shook her head. "She had some friends there who moved away. I don't think she would have walked that far."

"She probably just needs some time to think," I said, hoping it was true. "Time to be alone and process her thoughts."

The woman ran a hand through her hair. "Maybe we should get you to where you're staying tonight. Treha is staying in our extra room, but you're welcome to be on our couch. We have plenty of room."

"I couldn't impose. I saw a hotel not far back."

"It's not an imposition," Miriam said.

"I appreciate that. But I'm thinking of Treha. I think it would be better for her if I didn't stay with you. Maybe if we go back to Desert Gardens, she'll be there."

We drove back and helped Elsie inside. Buck hadn't returned but the person at the front desk said no one had seen Treha. Miriam asked me to wait while she helped Elsie to her room. The old woman was tired from the driving and needed a nap.

When Miriam returned, she took me into her office and closed the door, her face grave. "There's something you should know. It's about the lie that Treha says you told. It concerns Treha's father. . . ."

Startled, I could only nod for her to go on.

"You gave her a picture of him and a name. Treha has a friend at school who helped her find information about him."

"I assumed that at some point she would try to find out more. I could have helped her with that."

"You told her this man passed away twenty years ago."

"That's right."

Miriam's face contorted, lines appearing in her forehead.

"What is it, Miriam?"

"Paige, Treha's father is not dead."

I stared at her, frozen. "What do you mean? Of course he is. He died in a car accident shortly after he returned to the States."

"I don't know the details, but Treha is convinced that her father is alive."

I felt light-headed as I walked to the parking lot. I wandered around looking for my car, then remembered it was a rental. Where was my mind?

Treha had to be mistaken. Maybe her friend who did the online search was lying.

Then an even more frightening thought invaded. *What if she's right?*

The car was stifling and rolling the window down didn't help, so I started the air conditioner. It was a compact and the engine rattled and so did the air through the vents. Despite the heat, my hands shook as I dialed the number.

When I heard my mother's voice, I closed my eyes, hoping there was something more to the story, some kind of plausible explanation. "Mom, I need a straight answer about something."

"Paige, what's happened?"

"I'm in Arizona. I'm meeting with my daughter."

"Oh, honey. How did she — ?"

"I need you to listen. I need an answer."

"What in the world is this about?"

"I've just heard something that concerns me. About David."

Silence on the line.

"Treha is under the impression that he's still alive. She thinks I've lied to her about him."

A long pause. "How could she think that?"

"I'm not sure, but she and a friend came to that conclusion. I need to hear it from you. Is it true?"

"Paige, that was so long ago. I don't know if he's alive."

"What? You told me he had died in a car

accident."

"Yes, that was the information we had. At first."

The shaking in my hands got worse. "At *first*? Back up. How did you find out about his death?"

"I don't think bringing this up now can help —"

"Mom, is he dead?"

Another pause, then her voice emerged like a whining moan. "I thought he was. That's what we were led to believe. It's what the mission told us."

"What are you saying?"

"There were two different teams on that short-term trip. I don't know if you remember that. One worked at the mission and in our village, and the other was working on another island. We received word about a prayer request from the US. They asked us to pray for David Weber's family, as he had been killed in an accident. That's the information I had, and I told you that."

"But the information was wrong?"

"There were two Davids. One on each team. They got the last name mixed up. It was an honest mistake. We were finally notified of the error, but that was later, after you had left for the States."

I tried to speak through a clenched jaw.

"And you never thought it was important to tell me?"

"At the time, I thought you had been through enough. It felt better to leave things the way they were. For everyone."

"The letters from him. They stopped. But it wasn't because he had died. Did the letters actually stop?"

Silence.

"Mother?"

"Yes — he wrote you. A few more times, even after you left. I wanted to discourage him. I sent him a short note asking that he please stop. Saying that you had moved on with your life."

I was shaking my head — had been shaking it most of the time she talked, I realized. "I don't believe this. No wonder you didn't want me reaching out to Treha."

"Paige, we did this for your good. For David's as well."

"Did you tell him I was having a baby?"

"Of course not."

"Right, how foolish of me to think you'd do that. Mom, your whole life has been based on telling people the truth. How could you do this?"

Through the line I could hear gritted teeth and a stiff neck. "We were doing the best we could. We were trying to care for you after you'd made a mistake."

The bile rose, the indignation, the feelings of betrayal. "Do you know where he is?"

"No. I haven't concerned myself with finding out that information. I knew it would only bring heartache. And I caution you, Paige. Information like this can destroy a person's life, his family, his reputation."

"I have to go," I said. I hung up before she spoke again and sat there in the hot car wondering what to do, where to go, and if there was anything else I didn't know about my life.

Chapter 33

Treha

Treha sat alone outside an Olive Garden restaurant in a hot metal chair. There used to be a young man who worked here and was nice to her, gave her breadsticks, but she didn't see him. This was one place she could go to think and not have to buy anything. But the sun beat down and she tried to think of someplace else. She didn't want to go back to Desert Gardens and face her mother.

Treha pulled out her phone, disregarded the missed calls, and dialed Charlie, who said he would come get her.

"Don't tell Miriam where I am, okay?" Treha said.

"She doesn't know where you are?"

"No."

"All right, Treha. But don't you think she'll be worried?"

"I don't want her to know."

"She'll need to know before the end of the day, though. She won't leave there without you."

When Treha didn't respond, he said, "Okay, I'll be right there. Give me fifteen minutes."

He pulled up in front of the Olive Garden in twelve minutes, which made her think he had the drive timed. He unlocked her door and she slipped in beside him. The seats were leather and cold and felt good. Charlie had the talk radio station on but lower than usual.

"Were you trying to bake yourself out there?"

"No."

"Did you get something to eat?"

"No."

"Why were you there, then?"

"I had to leave. I had to go somewhere to think."

"I know exactly how that feels. Where do you want me to take you? You hungry?"

"Just take me home."

"All right."

He drove out of the parking lot and the radio talk overwhelmed her thoughts. Finally Charlie said, "Don't you think we should tell Miriam? She's going to wonder where you are."

"You can call her and tell her I'm okay."

"Good. Remind me to call as soon as we get home. Did something happen at Desert Gardens?"

"My mother came. From Tennessee."

"Really? That must have been a surprise and a half."

"It was."

"Why did she come all the way out here?"

"To talk to me."

"About what? Was it something she couldn't have said back there?"

"I don't know."

"What do you mean, you don't know?"

"I don't know what she wanted to say. I didn't stay to listen."

"Maybe she feels bad about not contacting you sooner."

"I'm sure she does."

"Maybe she wants to apologize."

"Maybe she wants everything to be okay and happy and she wants to be forgiven and act like nothing bad ever happened."

Charlie looked at her sideways. "Maybe." He drove in silence until they came to the subdivision where they lived. He pulled over to the side of the road where the mailboxes were and got out and checked the empty box. He got back inside but didn't put the car in gear.

"What's wrong?" Treha said.

"Nothing. I was just thinking. You know, Treha, you coming to live with us, you invading our lives like you did . . ."

"I invaded?"

"Let me finish. Invasion is not always a bad thing. You've really changed our marriage. Miriam and I are closer than we've ever been. We're on the same page about a lot of things. And it was you being here that forced us to deal with our . . . stuff."

"Why are you telling me this?"

"Because God has given you a gift. You are a gift to everyone you meet. And he wants you to use that gift. For others. And for yourself."

"This has something to do with my mother?"

"It does. What if your mother being in your life pushes you to become what God wants you to be, even if she is a little late to the party? What if she can help you as much as you've helped us?"

"I can't trust someone who doesn't tell the truth."

"Dr. Crenshaw didn't tell the truth about himself and you forgave him."

"That was different."

"Maybe. And maybe I'm overstepping. I've tried not to. You'll probably come to this on your own, anyway, but I think you ought to give her a chance."

Treha looked at him. "Did Miriam talk to you?"

"No."

"You haven't even met my mother."

"I'd like to."

"Maybe you wouldn't."

"Well, I like to think that people's lives are like stocks. Some are going up and some are going down, but the numbers don't tell the whole story. If she came all the way out here to see you instead of just calling or texting, I think that's a good sign. Maybe there's an explanation about her lie. Maybe she deserves another chance. Or at least, just to be heard."

Treha thought for a moment.

"I don't say much, Treha. You know that."

"I never thanked you for the card you gave me when I went away."

"I'm glad it meant something to you. And I meant every word."

"I still have it."

Charlie laughed. "That's good. That makes two, right?"

"Two what?"

"Two written things you've kept. My card and your mother's letter."

Treha didn't respond.

"Tell you what. I don't think I'll call Miriam. I think you should do that. Tell her you're safe at home and you would rather not see your mother tonight. It's entirely your decision."

"Why can't you call her?"

"Because it's not my call. And because I know how long you've looked for your mother, and this is no time to walk away from her. Treha, even if she's a no-good, lying, scheming thief, she's your mother. There's something you can learn."

Charlie drove up the driveway and into the garage. He hit the button for the garage door, but Treha sat in the car.

Chapter 34

Paige

That Treha's father was still out there breathing brought a new set of questions to a table already overflowing with them. Where was he? Was he married? Had he ever looked for me? Had he tried to reach out in any way over the years? Did he have children?

After a phone call from Treha telling Miriam she was all right and that Charlie had taken her home, Miriam invited me to dinner at her house but made no promises about the food or conversation with Treha. I was just glad Elsie wouldn't be there. She was a sweet woman but a bulldog when it came to Treha's future and my past.

I spent the afternoon at a hotel on Oracle Road making several calls, including an extended one with Anna Waddel at Bethesda. It took me a while to find her and even longer to convince her to reveal what she knew. I told her I had no computer with me and no access to one other than the business office of the hotel, and finally she rattled off a list of information gleaned about David that surprised me. She had more tidbits about the man's life than I could imagine, complete with what he now looked like, his marital status, and where he worked. The discovery that he was alive had sent my heart reeling. The news that he had married and had a family both comforted me and sent me on a path of self-pity. Why had things turned out so well for him? Why hadn't he ever contacted me? The questions were endless.

"How did you find all of this?" I said.

"Treha had a name and your old picture. On the back we had a date and the mission organization. I matched his name with some info from the organization and then followed the bouncing Facebook posts and voilà — instant invasion of privacy. The only thing I haven't found is a home address."

I thanked her and hung up with enough time to run to the grocery store to pick up something for the Howards. I settled for a fruit basket and flowers and found their home as the sun set red over the Catalina Mountains. I had no idea the sunset in Tucson could be so breathtaking.

Charlie met me at the door and I fell in love. He was so warm and inviting and had no questions, just a smile and a hug and a wide-open heart. His eyes bugged at the fruit basket and he ushered me inside. Miriam had stopped for chicken on her way home. She gave me a hopeful look with raised eyebrows as Treha walked down the hall. My daughter didn't make eye contact, but you can't have everything.

As the meal began, I thanked them for opening their home to me on such short notice. I had barely tasted the chicken when Treha spoke.

"Why did you lie to me about him?"

"Your father?"

She nodded without looking up.

"Treha, I was told that he had died. This was shortly before you were born. I had no reason not to believe the news."

"Oh, dear," Miriam said, her face pained.

I explained what my mother had told me, the mix-up of names and then the deliberate hiding of the truth from me, though I didn't say specifically who had hidden the truth. Thankfully, Treha didn't ask.

"So this was as much of a shock to you as it was to Treha," Miriam said.

I smiled ruefully. "*Shock* is a kind way to put it. All these years I've lived with his memory, with thinking of him as a young man. I can close my eyes and see his face, his smile, trapped in time. I thought he would always be that age." I tried to catch Treha's eyes, but she still wasn't looking at me. "Treha, now I understand why you would leave, why you felt like you didn't want to speak with me. I don't blame you. I thought you were having second thoughts about me being your mother."

"Did you ever try to make contact with his family?"

"No. Maybe I should have. At the time, I believed the love of my life was gone. And the baby that had been conceived from our relationship was leaving. I'd never felt so alone in my life."

My daughter picked at her chicken as if trying to decipher some kind of complex word puzzle hidden between the wing and the breast. Miriam watched her intently, and it seemed she was gauging whether to interject a question or remain quiet.

"Then he still has no idea about me," Treha said.

"We thought it best — your grandparents and I — not to tell anyone. Looking back, that was selfish."

Treha stared at her plate. "Do my grandparents want to see me?"

I smiled at her and tried to put a good face on it, but I was sure she could tell I was hesitating. "As I told you, my father isn't well. He doesn't understand much. My mother cares for him. I know they'll be excited to meet you. I would love to take you there. But I know we need to work things out between us."

"What's there to work out?" Charlie said. Miriam touched his arm and he looked at her. "What? Did I say something I shouldn't have?" He turned to Treha. "You thought your mother lied and you ran from her. Now you know someone told a lie, but it wasn't Paige. Your mother was a victim of someone else's lie. End of questions. End of anger toward her. Right?"

All I could hear was the clink of silverware on plates. And somewhere in a back room of the house, a talk radio station. And a passing jet heading for the stratosphere. And a dog in someone's backyard. And my heart pounding.

"I think we need to let Treha process this in her own time," Miriam said.

I made a sound of agreement. Then my daughter spoke.

"Charlie is right. I don't have any reason to be mad. You didn't lie to me. You didn't know my father was alive. I still can't understand why you didn't contact me. But you're here now."

I nodded. "Yes. I am. I'm here for the long haul. No matter what. For as long as you'll allow me in your life, Treha."

Treha stood. I thought she was going to run again, but she stayed. I wiped my hands with a napkin and glanced at Miriam. The woman shrugged and I stood. Treha looked at me and her eyes captured my heart. My wounded, wandering-eyed child stood before me and opened her arms.

I embraced her, held her, and the feeling was better than I imagined. It was different than at Bethesda. There, I had unveiled myself to her on my terms with my agenda. Now I was being freely embraced on her turf, by her choice.

When Treha pulled back, I saw pleading in her eyes. I thought she might ask me to return to Bethesda with her, to help her face the school and finish the semester. But instead, she said words I never expected to hear, words I had never considered.

"Will you take me to my father?"

I searched her face, and before I could think it through, before I could weigh the consequences or ramifications, I said, "Yes."

Chapter 35

Paige

We stopped for gas in Deming, New Mexico. Charlie had told me of a shortcut that would take some time off the drive. Instead of going all the way to Las Cruces, we could head northeast to Hatch and hit I-25. "They grow some awfully good green chiles in Hatch," Charlie had said. Treha said she wanted to stop on the way back and get some for him.

I used the restroom and bought some snacks and a cup of bitter coffee to keep me awake. The drive so far had been beautiful, though desolate. Places in eastern Arizona looked like the back side of the moon, or like John Wayne could come riding down one of the arroyos and cross the interstate in front of us and no one would blink.

For the most part, Treha sat in silence. I asked questions — if she wanted to listen to the radio, if she was too hot, too cold, needed to stop — but she seemed disinterested. So I turned the radio on low and kept quiet, resisting the urge to fill her silence with my chatter.

In the afternoon we made it to Albuquerque and I hit the regret stage. Why had I chosen to drive this distance in the small, noisy Toyota rental car? We could have flown to Colorado on a two-hour flight that would have put us within an hour of David. Somehow I'd thought this extended time alone would be good for us, and Miriam had agreed, but now I was second-guessing.

We drove another hour north and found a hotel hidden from the interstate in Santa Fe. The young man at the front desk wore a white shirt and tie, and he had an earring and hair tied in a ponytail. He smiled, glancing at Treha, and named a few nearby restaurants when I asked for a recommendation. When he said Chipotle was in walking distance, Treha asked if we could eat there. I was just glad she had a preference. He pointed the way and we walked, stretching our tired bodies.

"Did you see how that young man smiled at you?" I said as we crossed the parking lot.

"Men don't see me."

"I think he did. He thought you were cute."

"You can't know that."

"Not for sure, not unless I ask him. You wait here, I'll go back."

Treha grabbed my arm and I grinned as we kept walking. "You are a lovely person, Treha. You have to start believing that. You have to gain some confidence and pretty soon you'll be able to look up instead of down."

"So you don't like who I am."

"I love who you are. You don't have to change for me to love you. But since I've lost my classroom, at least for the time being, I might as well use my teaching ability to help you become all you can be. For example, you don't have your driver's license, do you?"

"No."

"Do you want one?"

"I don't need one. Miriam got me a state ID."

"But at some point you'll want to learn to drive, right?"

"It scares me to even think about."

"I was scared to come find you. I was scared to let anyone know I was your mother. So if I can do this, you can get your license, don't you think?"

"You're older than me."

"Don't let your youth hold you back. I'll help you. I'll bet Charlie will too. You'll be surprised how much the world will open up when you're able to drive. Able to go anywhere you want anytime you want."

"What if I fail?"

I shrugged. "I think failure is the exit ramp just before the town of success."

"Who said that?"

"I did, didn't you hear me?"

"I mean, whose quote is that?"

"It's nobody's — I made it up. And it's true. You take an exit, it's the wrong one. You turn around and get back on the highway. Sometimes when you fail, you're a lot closer to your destination than you think. The failure helps you understand this."

"That sounds like something I would read in a book."

"Think of it this way. What's the worst that can happen if you fail a driver's test? You go back and try again."

"I don't want to feel embarrassed."

"Treha, life is failure. One after another. If you never fail, it means you aren't trying enough new things."

"Is that what you believe or what you live?"

"It's an intellectual proposition most of

the time. But every now and then I have to actually live by it." I stopped her outside the restaurant. "We have so much to walk through together. So much to live. I don't want to miss anything, Treha. Not the failures or successes or anything in between."

Treha stared at me, her eyes moving slightly from side to side, then turned and walked inside. I took a breath and followed.

I figured we'd eat in the restaurant, but Treha wanted to go back to the hotel, so we got our food loaded up in a brown paper bag and walked back.

"How much farther do we have to go?" Treha said as we crossed the lobby.

"Colorado Springs is about five hours away. I figure we can get a good night's rest, have some breakfast, and hit the road. We'll be there tomorrow afternoon."

"Do you think he'll remember you?"

"I hope so. I'm sure he'll be a little surprised to see me. And more than a little shocked to meet you."

We rode the elevator to the third floor and returned to our room. Two double beds and a view out the window at Santa Fe that was almost as good as the Catalinas at the Howards' house.

Treha sat on the bed and ate while I

spread out a napkin on the round table in the corner. I spoke my next words to the wall as I opened the aluminum lid covering my food.

"Treha, I want to suggest one more time that we let him know. I don't think it's fair to him or his family that we just show up. Somehow it feels cruel."

"Is that why you drove instead of flying?"

I turned to her. "What?"

"Did you choose to drive so you could have more time to change my mind?"

Smart girl. I shouldn't have been surprised. "How did you come up with that theory?"

"Am I right?"

"Maybe. I guess I was hoping the drive would wear you down. You'd come over to the dark side of my viewpoint. But the main reason I wanted us to drive is so we could spend this time together, getting to know each other along the way." I could hear longing in my voice and hoped it didn't sound like desperation.

"I don't want him to know we're coming. I want to see him first."

"But we don't even know he's there. He could be on vacation. He could be on a business trip. Why don't you want him to know?"

"I want to see his face."

"You mean his reaction to you?"

"No. I want to see him before you tell him about me."

"But you have seen him. Anna said she showed you some of his pictures from Facebook."

"It's not the same." She put down her food and stared at the wall. Then she said, "I want to look at him and see if he is the kind of man who could love someone like me."

My breath left me and I put a hand on my chest. "Oh, Treha, I don't think there's anyone on the planet who couldn't love someone like you, if they get to know you."

Treha held the biggest burrito I'd ever seen to her mouth. "Isn't that what all mothers say?"

I smiled. For that one moment, it felt like we were moving toward something new, something good, and something frightening at the same time.

Getting ready for bed was a little awkward for us both. We watched some television, then turned it off and listened to the hum of the air conditioner on low, a masking noise that blocked out the traffic and our breathing.

The room had been dark twenty minutes

when Treha whispered, "Are you still awake?"

"Yeah. I don't sleep well when I'm not in my own bed. Even then . . ."

"You have trouble sleeping?"

"When my mind gets going, when I'm worried about something, it just takes over and I can't shut it down."

"That happens to me, too. Have you ever read a book all through the night?"

"Many times. Usually it's something old. *Jane Eyre. Middlemarch.*"

"*Jane Eyre* is my favorite. I've never read *Middlemarch.*"

"You have to. Oh, Treha, we should get the audio-book and listen to it in the car. It's just amazing. It's long, but amazing."

"I've done that too. Read a book all through the night."

There was a lilt to her voice that made me want to respond, to ask another question and keep her going, pull her further out, but instead I listened, the darkness enveloping us.

"But it doesn't matter when I go to sleep; I always wake up at first light. It's always been that way. Every day."

"I'll bet you get exhausted," I said.

"Sometimes when I lose myself in a book, it feels like I've gone to sleep there even though I'm awake. It still feels good to get up in the morning because I know I get to go back into the story again. Back in that dream."

"I like that. It's a good way to put it."

I stared at the red LED lights on the digital clock beside the bed until the numbers changed. When I closed my eyes, I could still see the numbers.

Treha yawned. "When you were younger, when I was only a few years old, did you talk to me?"

I turned toward her, even though I could barely make her out in the darkness. "Talk to you?"

"Did you ever say anything to me? Out loud?"

"I thought about you a lot and prayed for you, but I don't know that I ever spoke any words out loud."

"I did. I used to talk to you. At night. I would be alone in bed. I couldn't do it during the day when there were people around because they all thought there was something wrong with me. Like I was crazy. But at night I could whisper to you. Talk to you."

"Did I answer?"

"Sometimes I would imagine a conversation between us. I would imagine what you looked like. And that I could crawl into your lap and sit and you would hold me."

Her revelation startled me and it took me a moment to respond. "I'm sorry I never got to do that, Treha. I'm sorry I never took the chance."

"It's okay." I heard her shift in the bed, the covers rustling. "I used to take other people's stories."

"What do you mean?"

"I dreamed through the stories of the older people I met at Desert Gardens and their memories became mine. Dr. Crenshaw — he was one of them. When he was young, his parents took him to an ice cream shop and gave him to another couple. This was during the Depression and they were very poor and couldn't keep him. So they gave him to this family in the ice cream parlor."

"How awful."

"It became something I imagined for myself. That I was walking in with you, holding your hand. You were like an angel in a pretty dress, and when you got my ice cream and sat me down, you told me to wait. And you walked out in the sunlight and never came back. That's how I've always seen you."

I winced at the story. "Well . . . I've come back now, haven't I?"

"Yes."

I took a deep breath and a warmth spread through me, as well as unease. What I'd said about failure, that it was an exit ramp — I didn't know if that was true or just something I'd come up with to encourage my daughter. Could I live it? Could I risk failure? I didn't want to move too quickly, but here in the darkness I felt an opening, an opportunity.

"Treha, can I ask you something?"

"Yes."

"Did you just want to be held . . . when you were younger? Is that something that went away, or do you still feel like that?"

"I don't know."

"Not a good answer."

"I know you don't like those words, but sometimes they're the only ones I have."

"Okay. I can live with that. As a mother, I think I'm going to have to learn how to live with the 'I don't know.' "

"Do you think I will ever be a mother?"

"I hope so. I want to hold your grandchildren and read them stories. I want to see you walk down the aisle in a pretty white wedding dress."

"I don't think that will ever happen."

"Well, God has a way of surprising us, doesn't he?"

A long pause. "I don't know if my baby

will be like me."

I took a deep breath, fighting to keep my voice steady. "Treha, you will be a great mother. I can tell that. Any baby would be so lucky to have you as a mother. And you shouldn't worry about passing along something bad to your child. You have so much good to pass along."

Another long silence and the air conditioner clicked and moved to a lower frequency.

"What are you afraid of?" Treha whispered.

That question again. Before I could answer, Treha said, "Is it about losing your job? I heard you talking with Miriam about it."

"I don't know," I said.

There was a response from Treha's side of the room, not quite a laugh or even a chuckle, but a tuft of air recognizing the irony of my words. It was a wonderful sound, especially when I'd never seen her so much as smile. It was a start. A good start.

"My whole life has been teaching. Throwing myself into my students, into the subjects. I've never really known what it's like to take time off. To slow down and think and ask questions. I had a sabbatical last year to write, but all I could think about was you and the guilt and shame I felt. And the less I wrote, the more guilt I felt. It was like a death spiral.

"So I am worried about not teaching. But the bigger worry is missing what I'm supposed to do in the first place. You know? Missing whatever good thing God has in store for me that might feel awkward at the moment. Or hard."

"You mean me."

"You're one of the good things I know God has in store. Which doesn't mean it's going to be easy. I'm going to disappoint you. You're probably going to feel like you'd rather not have a mother like me. And that's okay. That's understandable because we're both human beings and we both will make mistakes . . ." I stopped, the trail of my thoughts leading to something unexpected.

"What?"

"I was thinking about my own mother. It's difficult to deal with the hurt I feel toward her. The things that happened or didn't happen between us."

"You have to forgive her, don't you?"

"I suppose so." I sat up in bed. "I can't believe this."

"What?"

"All this time I've thought it was about you forgiving me. About me pursuing you and you making the decision to move toward me. Daughter forgiving the mother who abandoned her. We're a lot more alike than you know, Treha."

I took a deep breath, steeled myself, and made the decision to try. Pulling back the covers, I swung my feet over the edge of the bed and stood.

"Where are you going?" Treha said.

"Scoot over. Your mother is going to give you a good-night hug."

I couldn't see Treha's face but as soon as I put my arms around her, I could feel the resistance, the tense muscles, the rigid back. I wanted to sing, do something motherly, but my mind went blank of all those nursery songs. Besides that, my daughter was twenty-two years old.

Instead, I kissed the top of her head and kept my arms around her. "Treha, I'm so sorry for the years we've missed. I don't think there are enough words in the English language or time left in my life to tell you how sorry I feel."

Treha had grown slightly less rigid but still seemed uncomfortable, so I squeezed her one last time and went back to my own bed.

"Good night, Treha."

■ ■ ■ ■

I fell asleep sometime after midnight and didn't wake until the sun peeked through the window blinds. I'd had a dream, something about David, him coming to me on the beach, holding out a hand, beckoning with a lover's eyes.

When I sat up, Treha's bed was empty and the room quiet. My heart sank. I had a terrible feeling that she was gone, that I had frightened her by reaching out.

I quickly dressed and found her in the breakfast room eating fruit and yogurt. We were back on the road by nine.

Chapter 36

Paige

One of the great philosophers said that life can only be understood backward but it must be lived forward. It felt like the same proposition driving to Colorado. No matter how long I studied the rearview, I had a winding road with plenty of traffic before me, a daughter beside me, and a lost love ahead.

Lost didn't quite capture it, nor *unrequited.* Disinterested, perhaps. David had given up — even if my mother had discouraged him, he could have pursued me. He could have followed up a year later, two years, ten. How could a good guy go that far with a young girl and just drop her?

Perhaps he was told *I* had died. Perhaps he got involved with someone else. Perhaps he never really loved me.

These were my thoughts, aided by Treha's silence as we drove. I learned they don't sell

Middlemarch at truck stops, so we had to wait.

The scenery changed as we rose in elevation from New Mexico into Colorado and through Pueblo. Pikes Peak stood like a white-capped beacon in the distance, and I wondered what settlers and natives had felt when they saw the mountain. Did it inspire awe or did they become used to the view?

The GPS took over as we hit Colorado Springs. I navigated from the interstate to a major side road with newer construction dotting the rolling, hilly landscape. We had both eaten so much at breakfast that we skipped lunch. I couldn't have eaten anyway, this close to our destination. I wondered if Treha felt the same way.

David now worked for a relief ministry that provided food, water, and the gospel to people who needed them. It fit with what I'd known of him years earlier — he had a heart for children and a desire to help heal the world. From what Anna had said, he held a communications position at the organization. I imagined him writing press releases, dealing with online issues and fund-raising. Maybe traveling to exotic destinations to get his hands dirty every now and then. I hadn't seen updated pictures — I'd avoided looking for them, truthfully —

but I imagined him aging gracefully, with more wrinkles when he smiled and a hint of gray. Maybe a few extra pounds. But he would have the same athletic build, the same calming, generous voice.

I found the redbrick building and parked across the street from the entrance, a good way from the main parking lot. In the distance we could see the Air Force Academy and pine trees engulfing the front range.

"Are you sure you want to do this?" I said.

Treha sat forward, scanning the parking lot. "That one right there. The white one. I think that's his car. I saw it in his pictures."

I pulled to a side street and parked under some trees that gave us shade and a little seclusion. "So your plan is that we wait until he comes out and spring it on him? You walk up and say, 'Hi, Dad'?"

"I told you, I want to see his face. I want to see how he walks. If he talks with the people he works with."

"And if he passes the test, then what?"

"I don't know yet. If you don't want to stay, you can leave me here."

Both of us were getting testy under the strain. At least she was showing some kind of emotion. But I tried to calm my tone.

"Treha, I'm in this with you. You're not

getting rid of me. I just want to be prepared in case the police come and ask us why we're spying on a parking lot. There are stalking laws, you know."

"The police have better things to do."

We watched the building and talked about where we might stay the night, where we might eat, what we could see while we were in this part of the country. I was fatigued from the drive but more nervous than tired. What would I feel when I saw him? Did I have a right to feel anything?

I had never been to Colorado and neither had Treha. I knew enough to tell her the skinny yellow-leaved trees were aspens, but that was about it. The sky turned from brilliant blue to slightly overcast with dark clouds rolling above us. At four thirty workers began to trickle out to the parking lot.

"I know I have to deal with my past, but is it fair to force someone else to deal with his?" I said. "This is a philosophical question, not an indictment."

"What do you mean?"

"I made a big mistake with David. I'm finally working through that. But once we see him, once we confront him, we're requiring that he face it too, ready or not. Is that fair to him?"

"I think that's him," Treha said, pointing.

"The one with the white shirt."

I wished we had stayed on the other side of the street. We were much too far away to see his face well, but I could tell from his gait that this was David. He walked in a loping, easy purchase as if the world were his personal treadmill. Long sleeves rolled up. Glasses now. I hadn't anticipated glasses but they looked good.

My cell phone rang and if our seat belts hadn't been fastened, we might have both jumped from the car. With my eyes on David, I answered.

"Paige, it's Ron."

I wanted to drop the phone or maybe throw it through the windshield. Why Ron? Why now?

"Ron." His name came out like an accusation and a little like an admission of guilt.

"I was worried about you after what happened at Millhaven. I just wanted to know you're okay."

"Yes. I'm okay. I'm doing well . . . I mean, I appreciate you caring enough to call. Thank you."

"Dr. Beckwith thought you might be in Arizona."

As he neared the parking lot, David stopped to talk with an older gentleman. He listened to the man as he talked, gesturing with his hands. Then David put his hand on the man's shoulder and I looked at Treha taking all of this in.

"I'm with Treha now, Ron. Some really good things are happening. Hard things, but good."

A sigh of relief on the other end. "That's what I was praying. That you two would connect, that there would be forgiveness and reconciliation."

"It's going to take some time, I think, but we're moving in the right direction." Suddenly I almost wished I could tell him more — that we could sit down for that coffee I kept promising and I could tell him everything.

"I'm so glad to hear that. And I'm praying about Millhaven, as well. They would be foolish to lose a great teacher like you. Someone who cares about her students."

David and the man stood in the shadow of the mountains, talking, the wind whipping up. He had less hair or it was cut shorter, and it was graying.

"Paige, you have people who really care about you. I'm one of them. If you need anything at all, please call. No strings. Okay?"

"Thank you, Ron. That's very kind."

When I hung up, Treha said, "Who is Ron?"

"He's a professor at Bethesda."

"Is he your boyfriend?"

David moved to his car, the white one, and got in.

"He wants to be. We've known each other a few years. He's very nice."

"But you don't love him."

"Can we talk about something else? Like what we're going to do about your father over there?"

Treha cocked her head toward me. "You said I could ask you anything. Talk to you about anything."

White lights and his car backed up.

"You're right. And I meant that. I'm just a little nervous about seeing *him* again. Apparently I don't multitask well when I see an old flame."

We watched the white car pull out of the parking lot and turn in front of us.

"Follow him," Treha said.

I didn't question her. I just started the car and pulled out — to the honk of a horn. I slammed on the brakes and a red truck nearly hit us. The truck came to a full stop and I tried not to look at the driver. I lifted a hand in a mea culpa and let him pass.

"You're going to lose him," Treha said.

I pulled out, making sure I looked behind us this time, and the red truck turned the same way David had gone, intentionally slowing, it seemed, in a passive-aggressive way, preventing us from catching him.

David drove quickly, zipping through intersections, always staying just out of reach. When the red truck finally turned, I thought we had caught him, but David accelerated through a yellow light and roared into the distance.

I looked at Treha and her face showed the pain of the near miss. What followed was the longest red light of my life. I accelerated through the green but there was no sign of the little white car. We drove through subdivisions, past parks and strip malls, to no avail.

"Are you hungry?" I said.

Treha stared into the distance and nodded. We were ordering sandwiches when I got an idea. We took our food to the car and I dialed Ron.

I asked if he was near a computer and gave him David's name and the information I had. "Could you see if you could find a home address, a phone number?"

"Sure."

Treha ate while I listened to Ron's fingers on the keyboard.

"You're in Colorado?" Ron said.

"Yes, we just drove up today."

"And who is this David you're searching for?"

It occurred to me then that I should've called someone else — anyone else — to help me. But my only choice now was to tell the truth. "Ron, I don't know how to tell you this. Treha's father wasn't deceased like I thought. David is Treha's father."

"What?"

"I wasn't lying to you. I really believed he was dead."

"And you're just dropping by to say hello?" There was hurt in his voice.

"No — well, I'm not sure." Suddenly the food we'd ordered didn't look appetizing. "If you'd rather not do this . . ."

"No, it's fine." His voice had grown a little colder, but he said the name of the ministry where David worked. "His address is not listed. But I used to know someone who worked with that organization. Let me call you back."

We ate in silence watching the traffic and the sun's golden glow on the mountains. I suddenly got the reference to "purple mountain majesties" just looking at the surroundings.

Twenty minutes later the phone rang and

Ron gave me an address. I punched it into the GPS as we talked. "It looks like we're about ten minutes from his house."

"Paige . . . I'm sorry. I'm sure you're just doing the best you can for Treha. Call me with anything you need. I'll be praying for you two."

"Better make it all three of us," I said. "And, Ron? Thank you."

We followed the directions and came to a nice subdivision with houses not too close together and signs that said Neighborhood Watch every few streets. Two-story homes with backyards filled with trampolines and playground equipment. Well-kept front lawns and lampposts near the mailboxes that I could imagine with red bows at Christmas. He lived on a wide street with sidewalks that looked like they stretched to Denver.

When the GPS informed us that we'd reached the destination, Treha leaned forward and studied the home. The two-car garage was closed and the driveway empty.

"I hope this is it," I said. "You want to go in?"

"Look at the mailbox," Treha said. Above it was the name *Weber.* "No. Let's wait."

"Wait for what?"

"Let's just wait."

I pulled into a nearby cul-de-sac where we had a good view of the house but were more inconspicuous. Treha finished her sandwich and watched the house. It felt like I was looking at the life I could have had if he had come back for me. There would have been no depression, no need for drugs. Treha wouldn't be damaged. With a sweep of the wand of time, all things could become new; everything could be made right in that alternate universe. But there is no magic wand that can change the past.

The sun continued its descent and still we saw no movement in the house. The car had developed that stale, we've-been-sitting-here-all-day-and-now-there's-food smell.

"Think I'll take a walk," I said.

I took the trash and Treha followed me around the corner and down the street toward a small park. She kept looking over her shoulder. I tossed the trash in a can, feeling freer than I had all day. Treha sat on a swing and I sat beside her.

"Why don't you like Ron?"

"I do. But I'm conflicted."

"Does he read books?"

"Lots of them. And he's conversant about great literature, which is a plus."

"Then why are you conflicted?"

"It's hard to explain. And if I did, I would

sound like a heel."

"A heel?"

"Uncaring. Too caught up in my own life. Persnickety, too. Picky. The truth is, I'm not sure there's any spark between us. No fireworks go off when I'm around him. That's not his fault, it's just the chemistry isn't there."

"Has he kissed you?"

I blushed and I'm not sure why; her question was as sincere and innocent as they come. "No."

"Then how do you know there are no fireworks?"

"He's not like that. He's not . . ."

"Like you felt with David?"

"I'm not comparing . . . at least not consciously. I thought David was dead, so there was no need to . . . no reason to wait for him."

"But with David there were fireworks. There was chemistry."

A mother walked up beside a young girl on a bike with training wheels. The girl got off the bike, removed her helmet, and began to run toward the swings but stopped when she saw us.

"It's all right, Valerie. We can go on the slide," her mother said.

"No, you can have my seat," I said, jumping up. Treha followed and we moved to a bench. The mother pushed the girl until she went higher and higher, squealing and giggling.

"I never got to do that with you," I said. "I never got to push you on a swing set or give you a birthday party."

"Go back to my father. There were fireworks. You loved him."

"Yes. As much as I knew about love back then." Finally I realized there was more here from Treha than simply interest in my sexual past. "Why are you asking?"

"I've always wondered if my mother and father loved each other. I used to think you got rid of me because you didn't love me. You didn't want me. Now I know that's not true. But if he had known about me, do you think he would have wanted me?"

"From what I knew of David, yes, I think he would have wanted to be your father."

We watched the mother and her daughter swing and laugh and play. I tried to blame the ache inside me on the altitude but knew better.

We walked slowly back to the car as dusk fell. Garages opened and trash cans were wheeled to the curb. There were no lights on in David's house.

"What are you thinking?" I said when we

were back in our seats.

She shrugged. "I'm thinking I'm tired. That we came a long way for nothing. And that I feel bad for Ron. He likes you but he doesn't have a chance."

To avoid looking at her, I fussed with the GPS, searching for a nearby hotel. "He has a chance, Treha. It's just that my life is a little complicated. Once things settle down . . ."

She interrupted me by putting a hand on my shoulder. A minivan pulled into the driveway and the garage door opened. We watched, breathlessly, as the van parked in the immaculate garage. A workbench. Bikes hung on racks. A lawn mower in its stall and other yard equipment. A water softener, a freezer. The American dream.

A woman got out of the driver's side and the doors behind her opened. A young boy jumped down holding a piece of paper that looked like a coloring sheet from a restaurant. Two older girls followed the boy inside. Then the white car pulled in beside them and David got out and opened the back of the minivan, taking out a plastic bag with what looked like Styrofoam boxes inside. A small dog met David at the door, wagging his tail, and then the garage door closed like a curtain on the scene.

"He must have met them somewhere," Treha said. "That's why he was driving so fast."

He was eager to get to his family, I thought. *Eager to meet them and have dinner.*

"What do you think?" I said. "It's your call. Do you want to talk to him?"

"Let's go to a hotel," Treha said.

I pulled away from the curb, looking carefully again for oncoming traffic, and paused by David's driveway. Instead of visiting a grave, I was outside his home — a much better shrine to love than a tombstone. Though it was hard to wrap my mind around him carving out a life with someone else, I would much rather have the perceived "love of my life" still walking the planet, happy with his family.

I must've pondered a bit too long because light illuminated the reflector on the mailbox and instead of a red truck bearing down on us, there was a rattle of wheels and light coming from the garage. Around the white car came David in that generous loping walk, pulling two trash cans toward the curb.

"Go," Treha whispered urgently.

I pulled forward a few feet and stopped.

"Get out of here. He's coming. He'll see us."

There are moments in life you wish you

could relive, and I had the feeling this would become one of them. Years down the road, I would want to come back to this curb and keep my foot on the brake. It's how I felt about the birth of my daughter. I wish I'd said something to David, given him a chance twenty years ago, been stronger with my mother and father. Treha kept urging me forward but I couldn't leave. Something held me there.

I put the car in park and watched David roll the recycling container to the curb and then position the other can a precise distance away. He straightened the containers, mashed the lids down, and went to the mailbox, right behind our car. He removed letters and walked toward the house.

Treha sat rigid, not even daring to look in the side mirror. "Please, let's go. Hurry!"

I unlatched my seat belt, opened my door, and stepped out. The light came on inside the car and a bell dinged that my keys were still in the ignition.

Treha grabbed my arm and gave me a look of sheer terror as if we were in a horror movie and I was intent on going to the basement. "Please," she begged. "Let's go."

It was this glance at my daughter, at her face and all that she had carried her entire life, that compelled the door closed and my seat belt back in place. I reached for the gearshift.

Something tapped at my window and my heart raced. Treha flinched. David stood on the other side of the glass, bent over, a quizzical look on his face.

"Just drive," Treha whispered.

I pulled the lever into drive and he stepped back.

"Can I help you?" he said. His voice was muffled by the window, but it was still his voice. Like a melody from some forgotten song that arrests you and takes you right back to where you were the first time you heard it. The first time he said my name, my insides had been like jelly. The first time he said he loved me, I felt whole and free. And now here he was again, years later and with three children of his own.

His eyes looked the same, even behind the glasses. Amazing.

The light had faded to black inside the car. I put the window down halfway and looked at him, his face silhouetted by an overhead streetlight. "We're fine, thank you."

"Are you sure?" he said with a hint of doubt.

"Yes. My daughter and I were just . . . driving around."

He nodded and dipped his head to look at Treha. She kept her face angled away like a kidnapped child. "Okay," David said, smiling. Dimples in his cheeks. Those cute ears of his that hugged his head and pointed a little at the top like an elf's. Treha had those ears. "Just wanted to make sure."

He put his left hand on the top of the window and I saw the ring, the thick wedding band that brought a wave of regret. As he walked away, I glanced in the rearview. He leafed through the mail by the light of my taillights.

"You got to hear his voice," I said to Treha. "I wanted you to hear it."

"Why didn't you go?"

"I couldn't. I had to speak with him, at least once."

"You think he recognized you?"

"No. It's been too long. Too much time and distance and wrinkling skin on my face. How did you like him? Did he seem like someone who would love you?"

"I liked him fine. Can we please leave?"

I let my foot off the brake and had started to pull out when I heard the voice again.

"Paige?"

The window was still halfway down. I stopped. David moved to my window and squatted by the car, allowing the light to shine on my face this time.

"Paige Redwine. It is you. I can't believe this. It's been . . . half a lifetime. What are you doing here?"

"I'm not entirely sure." My voice shook as I spoke the words. I hadn't prepared for this and when he continued, I felt relieved.

"Somebody in the office today asked if I'd seen the video — you talking with your daughter at the school. And I said, 'I know her. I met her on a mission trip more than twenty years ago.' " He put a hand to his head. "I can't believe this. You're in front of my house. That's crazy. What are you doing here?"

Treha leaned toward me. "I told you we should have gone. Please. Let's go."

David looked at me, saying something with his eyes, but I couldn't decipher the message with Treha pulling me in the other direction. I turned to her. "Give me a minute."

I stepped out, barely remembering in time to put the car back in park, and closed the door. David started to hug me, but I extended a hand.

"It's good to see you," he said.

"David, I think it might be better if we came back another time. For some reason Treha doesn't . . . She's not comfortable."

"I understand. That's fine. Just stay right here and let me get my wife. She won't believe it."

"David." I said it forcefully, just hard enough to get him to step off the world he was in so he could move into mine. "You know Treha is my daughter, right?"

"Yeah, I told you I saw the video."

I searched his eyes. "She wanted to come to Colorado to see her father."

He squinted at me and cocked his head. "Okay. So her dad lives here?"

"David, Treha is twenty-two. I met you on the island twenty-three years ago."

The eyes said it all. Everything starts in the eyes. The color drained from his face, his mouth dropped, the cute dimples disappeared, and he looked at the pavement, searching for something in the asphalt he would never find.

I moved toward him in a gesture of comfort. I'd had twenty-three years to prepare for this moment, but it was something he stumbled upon taking out the trash.

He looked up at me. "What do you want?" His voice turned to gravel. "What does *she* want?"

I struggled to breathe. "You think I brought her here to punish you? I can assure you there's nothing further —"

"You must want something if you're sitting outside my house. Were you waiting for us to get home?"

"David, we don't want anything. You had no idea about her. I know that. We never told you, so you couldn't have known."

"But you're telling me now. How could you do this, Paige? Show up and drop this?" His voice was louder now, a vein in his forehead surfacing.

The front door opened and a young girl stuck her head out. "Daddy, come inside!"

"I'll be right there, honey," he called.

Voices from inside. Then the girl said, "He's talking to some lady," and the door closed. The front window blinds lifted and I looked away.

David ran a hand through his hair. "Why didn't you tell me? This is not fair. You can't do this to me. Not now."

"I thought you were dead. That's what I was told. That you were in an accident. And I . . ." I put my hands on my head and pressed down. "I've made a mess of things. I'm sorry. I'm really sorry, David."

I got back in the car.

"Paige, wait."

I got one more view of David in the rearview before we sped out of the neighborhood. He was standing in his driveway with the mail in his hand and a look on his face I'd never forget.

Chapter 37

Paige

We found a hotel near I-25, across from a theater and a huge church. Nearby was a grocery store and we bought some water and fruit in a plastic container. When we passed a large bookstore, I made a U-turn and went inside. Treha opted to stay in the car.

I came back with a copy of George Eliot's *Middlemarch.* "They didn't have an audio edition, but you can start this anytime you want."

Treha took the bag and pulled out the hardcover "classic" edition. She seemed glad to have something to look at while we drove back to the hotel. It gave her a reason not to look at me — not that she was doing that anyway.

We ate our fruit in the breakfast area with the TV on, a sports channel blaring highlights of the latest football games. Treha and

I were the only ones there but neither of us had the energy or desire to turn down the volume.

Up in our room, I came from the bathroom and found Treha staring at the television. She'd found a news program about a crime of passion and the resulting trial accusing the husband. Bloodstained carpets, photos of the smiling victim with her husband, and troubling questions were all described by a smooth-voiced reporter. He tied the story together with interviews of skeptical family members as well as the husband in a prison jumpsuit.

Finally I couldn't take any more and turned off the TV. "I think we should talk."

Treha picked up the remote and turned the TV on again.

I returned to the bathroom to regroup. All evening I'd tried to give Treha her space, but that was getting us nowhere. So maybe it was time for another approach.

I strode back into the room as the show went to commercial and unplugged the power cord, then stood in front of Treha's bed. "I think we should talk."

"I don't want to talk."

"Why not?"

"Because I don't want to."

"Treha, it's okay to be angry with me. I

can handle it."

Treha picked up the book by the side of the bed and opened to the first pages.

"Treha."

The girl looked up. "You can't unplug this." She turned and faced the wall.

I sank onto my own bed. "Fine. We won't talk, then."

I shuffled desperately through my meager mental supply of parenting wisdom. I'd heard someone say that even if teenagers pushed you away, they really wanted you with them. Treha wasn't a teenager, of course, but maybe the principle was the same.

It took ten minutes that felt more like an eternity. But after ten minutes, Treha mumbled something.

"What was that?"

"I wanted to see if he did it."

"Who?"

"The man on TV. The husband."

"I think our lives are more interesting. There's no blood on the carpet but it is a pretty engaging story."

More silence and a page turn. Finally Treha rolled onto her back and stared at the ceiling. "I don't understand why you didn't leave. You said this trip was up to me. The decision was mine. And when I told you to go, you sat there."

I nodded. "I knew you wanted to leave. I understood that. But something took over when I saw him. I felt that was our best chance — my only chance to make contact. If I didn't do it then . . ."

"But you didn't care how I felt."

"I do care. But this is something I'm learning, Treha. And it's a hard lesson. If I had listened to my gut when you were born, if I had done what I wanted to do, I wouldn't have let you go. I think God was trying to break through to me, but I wouldn't listen. And right then, when David approached us, I felt it was right to stay, to get out and talk with him."

"Then I can't trust you."

"That's not true. You can trust me. I'm committed to doing everything I can with your best interests at heart. But sometimes what I think is best and what you think is best will conflict. Trust is not a one-way street. And it's built over time. You have to believe that I want the best for you and pray I'll make wise decisions, just like I have to believe that about you."

Treha sat up on her elbows. "This is not how I thought having a mother would be."

"What did you think it would be like?"

"I thought we would talk and share stories.

That I would feel all warm inside when I heard your voice."

"You don't feel that?"

"Not now."

I tried to stifle a smile. And I risked moving to sit on Treha's bed. "My inclination is to try to make you happy. Just do everything you want. Even driving up here was that. I thought I could show you how committed I was by doing this. It's like a divorced parent who comes back into a child's life with presents and trips to the amusement park every weekend. I don't want to buy your love, Treha. I want to do what's best for you, for both of us."

"And if I think what's best is different, you ignore me?"

"That's what we have to work through. This is not easy. It's messy. But in the end, I think it's going to be good for —"

The room phone rang, a rattling, warbling electronic sound that had been turned to its loudest setting. I answered and heard the sounds of football in the background.

"Ms. Redwine, it's Kathy Weber. David's wife."

"Hello."

"I'm in the lobby. Could you come down?"

In the lobby? *This* lobby? "How did you

find us?"

"David called around to different hotels. It didn't take long."

"He didn't come with you?"

"I can explain if you'll come down."

I gave a heavy sigh. "Okay."

"Who was it?" Treha said when I hung up.

"David's wife is here. She wants to talk to me."

"I don't want to go."

"I understand." How could I not? I didn't want to go either.

I plugged in the television and grabbed a key card. "I'll be back."

Kathy Weber had long, blonde hair with highlights. She looked like something out of a modeling magazine, but the makeup couldn't hide the pain on her face. I wondered how I would have reacted if our roles were switched — my husband's old lover surfacing. Would there have been blood on the carpet somewhere?

We shook hands awkwardly and sat at a small, round table.

Kathy began to speak, then stood and found the remote for the television and muted the sound. "This is awkward for both of us."

"Very. I'm sorry to put you in this situation."

"David and I have been through a lot in the past few years. This new revelation, you and your daughter coming here, felt like one more . . . I don't know, one more shoe dropping. It caught me off guard." She fiddled with her wedding ring, and I saw tears filling her eyes. "David told me there had been others. He mentioned you. But he never said there was a baby. Is it true he didn't know?"

"Our family kept that secret from everyone. I regret that. I think we all do."

"You never thought about telling him? You never tried to get in touch with him?"

"I was told that David had died. It was a misunderstanding at first, miscommunication from the mission field. And then it was simply a truth I was never told."

The answer seemed to calm the woman, but the tears didn't go away.

"I struggled with coming here," I said. "Treha wanted to see her father. Just look at him. She has this way of approaching life that's a little hard to grasp. And when we saw David, she asked me to leave. She didn't want to talk."

"But you stayed," Kathy said.

"Yes. I froze."

"Why?"

"I felt like it was a chance to finally tell the truth. Staying, talking with David, was just the right thing to do tonight. Talking instead of hiding."

"You're not the first to come back," Kathy said. "That's why he asked what you wanted."

"I don't understand."

"David was unfaithful to me." Kathy said it with a puckered chin. She took some tissues out of her purse. "We're working through that. We've been working through that for a while."

"I'm sorry." It was the only thing I could think to say. If David could have an affair with a wife who looked like this, what hope was there for any marriage?

"He's battled some serious temptations through the years. Perhaps it's better to say he hasn't battled well. But I think he really wants the marriage to work. He says he's committed to doing . . ." She paused and wiped her eyes. "I don't know why I'm telling you this."

"You thought I might be making a play for your husband," I said. "I can understand that."

"I don't know what I thought."

"I can assure you I'm not here to renew a

relationship. Finding Treha has sent me on this journey I never expected. I reached out because of her. Only because of her."

"But if you thought he was dead until recently, isn't there part of you that . . . ?"

I leaned forward. "Kathy, I'm not interested. Period. What happened feels like another life. I'm not a threat." As I said it, I knew it was the truth. The David I remembered didn't exist in this world.

"Thank you for that," Kathy said. "That's reassuring. But what about your daughter? I'm not sure what we can offer as a family. . . ."

I nodded. "Treha's financial needs are covered. I'm hoping she'll want to stay with me. It's still early in the game — I've only recently met her too, and there's so much we haven't figured out. I honestly think just knowing her dad exists is enough for her."

Kathy wadded the tissues tightly in one hand. "I'd like to meet her at some point. It's just that now doesn't feel . . ."

"I understand."

"Maybe down the road?" Kathy said without hope in her voice. "I just can't imagine bringing her into our family right now."

I studied the woman's face. "You need time. I've had years to respond to this and it's been so hard. I'll help Treha understand. She'll be fine. Relieved."

Kathy gathered her things and rose. She gave me a polite hug and walked out the door.

Chapter 38

Paige

On the drive back to Arizona, Treha told me a story she had heard from a man speaking in chapel about a sick mule near death. The farmer, thinking the animal had died, shoved him into an old well and began burying him. The mule, awakened by the fall, stood and, as every shovelful of dirt hit him, shook off the dirt and stepped up on the pile. Eventually the mule used the dirt meant to bury him to climb out of his pit.

"You got to shake it off," Treha said, imitating the man who had spoken.

I chuckled. But at the same time I was thinking that's what David and Kathy were trying to do. And so was Treha. So was I.

With these thoughts came the realization that if Treha could shake off her past and step up, I could do the same. The past is like grace. It's not enough to know *about* it. We all know what happened back there.

Grace allows you to see yourself in light of the past, not in the shadow of it. You see the truth about yourself, your need. On that drive toward Tucson, the past began to lose its grip on my soul.

Miriam organized a going-away party at Desert Gardens. Elsie was much warmer toward me. She took me aside and gave me a pep talk about becoming Treha's mother.

"It's not your right, it's something you earn," Elsie said. "You keep Treha's best interests at the front and you won't go wrong. And you should speak with Miriam. She's been the closest thing to a mother that girl has ever had."

When I had Miriam alone in her office, I told her how much I appreciated all she had done for Treha. "I want you to be as much a part of her life as you want to be."

"As she wants me to be," Miriam corrected.

"Yes, of course."

"It took courage for you to move toward her. To come out from the shadows. You will need more for the days ahead."

"One step at a time, right?"

"Yes. With Treha it will be slow, deliberate steps. You're going to be a different woman because of her, Paige. You know that?"

"Yes."

"Listen to her. She will tell you things without you knowing."

I thought about Miriam's words as we listened to *Middlemarch* together on the plane ride. There were tears in my eyes when we finished. Treha looked out the window and took out her earbud, just staring at the clouds.

I replayed the last paragraph again for myself:

> Her finely touched spirit had still its fine issues, though they were not widely visible. Her full nature, like that river of which Cyrus broke the strength, spent itself in channels which had no great name on earth. But the effect of her being on those around her was incalculably diffusive: for the growing good of the world is partly dependent on unhistoric acts; and that things are not so ill with you and me as they might have been, is half owing to the number who lived faithfully a hidden life, and the rest in unvisited tombs.

Eliot was right. And as I thought about my own contribution to the planet, my shouting into the void, I saw that my unhistoric act of moving toward my daughter was part of the courageous legacy I might leave. The best "hidden" life was lived in full exposure to those I loved.

It was toward another set of hidden lives that we were compelled on what I believed was the last leg of our journey, or at least this first journey together. I had phoned my mother and told her I was going to take Treha back to Tennessee and sort through the issues surrounding my teaching and moving ahead with life, but she gave an invitation I couldn't refuse.

"Come here, Paige," she said. "Your father is not well. He's agitated and drawing into himself. It may be your last chance. It may be *her* last chance . . . Treha's, I mean. We can help with the tickets."

Hearing my mother say her granddaughter's name was enough. But I wasn't idealistic about the visit. I knew it wouldn't be easy. In fact, the prospect of Treha meeting her grandparents made the trip to Colorado look like a picnic.

Treha was visibly nervous, probably sensing my tension. "Do I look like them?" she said as we waited in the aisle to deplane.

She had her hair pushed behind one ear, and her facial structure and ears looked so much like David's that I couldn't help but smile. “You have my father’s love of words, that’s for sure.”

“And his eyes? You said that once.”

“Yes, and his eyes.”

“Is your mother really okay with me coming?”

“If she’s not, it’s too late now,” I said. Then I put an arm around her. “She’s going to love you, Treha.”

“What should I call her?”

“Call her whatever you feel comfortable with. Grandmother, Grandma, Mrs. Redwine. Or nothing at all. She’s invited you to see your grandfather. She wants you there.”

A friend of my mother’s met us at the airport and drove us to the house. She was pleasant but prepared us for the worst. “I wouldn’t expect too much from either one of them. The stress has been unbearable on your mom, Paige.” The way she said it sounded like a friendly warning instead of an accusation. That Treha had worked with older people gave me hope that nothing we encountered would shock her. In fact, I would probably lean on her.

My mother’s friend let us out in the driveway and watched us walk to the door. The moment we entered the house, it felt like we were in an alternate universe. It was the stillness that arrested me. Like a funeral waiting for the organ prelude.

Mom hugged me and I hugged her back. The trip with Treha and the invitation to bring her had helped temper my anger, at least a little. We'd have to deal with the truth, over time, but I kept the advice from Miriam and Elsie at the forefront. Do what was best for Treha. Let her meet her grandmother.

After the embrace I stepped aside and ushered my daughter forward. "Mom, I want you to meet Treha."

Treha stared at the floor. My mother looked at her, reaching out with misty eyes before her hands followed. But before she could embrace her, there came a muted wail that led to racking sobs, and she wobbled and put her hands to her face, over her glasses. Tears flowed like a swollen stream. My mother had always been the picture of composure and control, but the weight of the emotion drove her to the ground, and she reached out for support as she slipped to her knees in front of Treha with me trying to hold her steady.

My daughter knelt on the floor with my mother and it was more than I could take. Treha patted my mother's shoulders and arms, cocking her head and making a *shhh* sound. There were no words. Sometimes, I have found, you don't need words. The heart is enough.

When my mother had recovered, she stood and cradled Treha's face, shaking her head and looking at me as if she couldn't believe what she'd missed. Then she said, "Come in here, honey. I want you to meet your grandfather."

For a woman who once couldn't speak her granddaughter's name, it was quite a transformation. I didn't know what had happened in my mother's heart, but at that moment, I didn't care. She took Treha by the hand and led her into the living room, which had been converted into my father's personal hospital. A metal bed with railings and the accoutrements of convalescence. A box of plastic gloves and bottles of medicine and adult diapers and the smell of alcohol. All the old furniture had been shoved into a corner. My father sat like a statue in a mechanical chair, staring out the window as if he were in the stands waiting for a game that would never begin.

My mother brought Treha around in front of him, like a child who wanted to show off a new puppy. She leaned down to his face. "John, this is your granddaughter. Treha has come to visit us."

Treha knelt and put a hand on his armrest. His head didn't move, his eyes didn't follow her, but Treha seemed unconcerned as if she had seen this a thousand times.

"Hello, Mr. Redwine," she said softly. "Hello, Grandfather."

She touched his arm and then a shoulder and spoke gently, whispers I couldn't hear. There was no response, no eye movement or recognition like I'd seen in the documentary. Part of me had hoped that Treha would come into our lives and call him back to us and we would be whole again, a family, connected. But to be honest, I didn't have the faith to believe it could happen. My father was too far gone. He had launched out onto his own sea and the sails had disappeared over the horizon.

My mother stood beside me and hugged me, still weeping. "You brought her home, Paige."

"It's been such a long journey."

"For all of us," she said. She looked at me. "We're all guilty, aren't we?"

"And we're all forgiven," I said, and I could tell, deep in her heart, she knew I meant it. Thank God for mercy and forgiveness, even though it makes your face puffy.

That tender moment was broken by a shriek from my father. His arms flailed and

Treha fell back against the wall, her head hitting the window trim. It took my father three pushes to make it out of the chair, but before my mother or I could snap out of our shock to reach him, he was walking stiff-legged toward the stairs.

CHAPTER 39

Treha

Treha put a hand to her head and tried to get up, but the room spun. Her grandmother was on one knee, peering into her face. "Are you all right, honey? Did you hit your head?"

There were squiggly lines in her field of vision, but Treha made it to her knees and looked across the room at her mother wrestling with the old man — that was the only way she could describe the struggle. He was reaching out, trying to grab something, and her mother had her arms wrapped around his shoulders.

"Dad, you can't go up there!"

He didn't speak, didn't yell; he just fought, resolute in his desire.

Standing, Treha saw the gate at the bottom of the stairs, the kind used to block pets or young children from a fall or climb. The old man grabbed for it. He turned to

Paige and with both hands pushed her away, a wild look in his eyes.

"This is how he gets," her grandmother said, her voice trembling. "I can't control him."

Paige staggered backward and her father took the gate and tore it loose, scarring the wall and railing.

"Let him go, Paige. Just let him go!"

Like a man walking on stilts, the old man took the steps one at a time, looking at his feet, breathing heavily, a death grip on the railing. He looked like a toddler on a trapeze. Treha's mother gathered herself and followed, ready to catch him. When he made it to the top, he swayed backward and for a moment it looked like they would both tumble. Treha hurried to them, her grandmother right behind her. The old man regained his balance and continued.

"Where's he going?" her grandmother said.

"Toward the office, I think," Treha's mother said.

"Let him go, then. When he's in there, close the door and hold on to it so he can't get out. I'll call the home nurse."

Treha followed her mother to the office door. It was open just a crack and they could see her grandfather moving around inside. Locking him in there didn't seem like a good idea, but wrestling with him seemed out of the question. His strength was surprising.

"What if he tries to break a window?" Treha's mother yelled.

"He won't. He'll just rummage around. He's done it before."

Treha heard her grandmother pick up the phone and speak with someone. She closed her eyes. The squiggly lines were still there but better.

"I'm sorry about this," Paige said. "Are you all right?"

Treha nodded. "That's never happened. The people at Desert Gardens got upset, but I was always able to calm them."

"It's almost like you had the opposite effect here," her mother said absently, looking through the door again.

"Can I go in? I want to try again."

"I don't think you should. Let's contain him and let him cool off."

"What's he doing?"

"He's over by the closet for some reason."

"The nurse is on his way," Treha's grandmother said, holding her chest as she came up the stairs.

Behind the door Treha heard a thump, then a crash.

"Oh, John, no," her grandmother said.

They found Treha's grandfather on the floor, his arms up in the air and his feet moving as if he were still climbing the stairs. A box lay beside him, one edge crumpled from the fall.

When he noticed them there, fire ignited in his eyes and he rolled over and pushed himself up until he could stand, then turned to the closet and reached high for the shelf.

"What's he looking for?" Treha said.

"God only knows," her grandmother said. "John, please stop. Please come over and sit down before you hurt yourself."

He shook his head as if he understood the words but kept clawing at the shelf above the hanging clothes. Another box clattered down, bouncing across the room.

"Dad, stop it! You're going to get hurt."

"I'll see if the nurse is here," Treha's grandmother said. "Just try to stay out of his way."

"He's looking for something," Treha said to her mother.

"He probably thinks he's back in New Guinea. That he has more translation work to do." She moved to the desk and brought back a leather Bible and held it out to him. "Dad, is this what you're looking for? See?

You finished. You completed the whole thing."

He stared at the book, then pulled a wheeled chair from the desk and tried to raise a foot to stand on it.

"Dad, no! You're going to break your neck."

Paige pulled the chair away and the man gritted his teeth.

Treha touched her mother on the arm and moved past her with a different chair, sturdier, wooden. Four legs with no wheels.

She put a hand on her grandfather's shoulder. "Let me help. Whatever you're looking for, I can get it for you."

Still breathing heavily, he looked at Treha. His breathing slowed and his muscles relaxed.

"Is it still up there?" Treha said, coaxing him closer. "The thing you're looking for?" She rubbed his arm with one hand and looked into his eyes. "Do you want me to find it?"

His lips pressed together and opened. Then he did it again. A sound emerged like from an infant learning to make noise. "Buh . . . buh . . . buh . . ."

Treha put both hands on his arms, rubbing gently, looking deeply into his eyes. In her peripheral vision she saw her mother put a hand to her mouth.

"What's in the closet? What are you looking for, Grandfather?"

More consonants came rat-a-tat-tat from his lips, the *b*'s like a repeating rifle. "B-b-b-b-b-b-b-b . . ."

Finally he stopped and took a breath and looked directly at Treha. "Box," he said, elongating the vowel. When he got it out, he smiled like it was a splinter stuck in his brain that he had tried to remove for decades. The familiar logjam she had seen break and open a cascade of words.

"Good," Treha said. "A box. But there are a lot of boxes. Tell me when I find the right one."

She stood on the chair and her head barely reached the level of the shelf. Her arms were short and she had to stand on her tiptoes to reach what had been stored so many years.

"Let me do that," her mother said. "My arms are longer." She climbed onto the chair and pulled out a shoe box and held it up.

"Is that the box?" Treha said to her grandfather.

A blank stare on his face but his tongue touched the roof of his mouth as he blinked and struggled to speak.

"Try another one," Treha said.

Paige pointed at a bigger box. When there was still no response, she tried to move it, but it was stuck, wedged between the ceiling and something underneath. She moved the chair closer and managed to get her hands under the box. After several tries she scooted something small and wooden to the edge of the shelf and extracted it.

"It's my keepsake box," she said. "He made this for me from a tree that grew in our backyard. I didn't know we still had this." She held it out so Treha could see the intricate design of a tree near a stream and her name carved at the top.

Treha's grandfather grabbed the box so quickly that her mother stumbled, the chair tipped, and she fell into the shelves, barely able to catch herself.

Treha was there in a flash, holding her until she could right herself. "Are you all right?"

"I'm fine," her mother said, glancing at her father. He had the box at his desk, running his hands over the dust and clearing it away.

"The nurse is almost here," Treha's grandmother said, walking tentatively into the room. She stared at her husband hovering over the wooden box. "John?"

He put it on the desk, grabbed the wheeled chair, pulled it to himself, and fell in. Wrinkled hands lifted the top open and the other three in the room crept closer.

"What did you keep in there?" Treha said.

"My journal — there it is. That's my first journal. Mom, I had no idea you still had this."

"I didn't know it was here either."

There were ancient birthday cards, pictures of Treha's mother as a child, a pendant that she said her father had given her on her sixteenth birthday, a ring, as well as a collection of coins from other countries scattered at the bottom.

The old man moved the journal and pulled out a long, velvet pouch tied at the top. He removed it with shaking hands and sat back.

"What in the world do you have there, honey?" his wife said.

His breathing grew more rapid and his hands shook. He ground his teeth and began making a low, guttural sound like some frightened woodland animal caught in a trap.

Treha touched his shoulder. "It's all right. You found it. Do you want me to open it for you?"

His head wobbled like a bobblehead doll.

He gave a hint of a smile. Just the slightest rise of his upper lip over worn teeth. Then he placed the pouch in Treha's hands.

"What's he doing?" her grandmother whispered.

Treha looked at her mother, who couldn't speak or breathe. Her grandfather was calm, almost expectant as he watched. Treha knelt in front of him and untied the leather cord that held the pouch tightly closed. When it opened, she pulled out a wooden ink pen, the same kind Treha had seen her mother carry.

A single word was carved into the wood.

Treha.

She looked up at the old man, then at her mother. "How long has this been in there?"

Her grandmother held out a hand. "Let me see that." She studied the pen. "He had to have made this years ago, when we were still . . . John, is this what you've been looking for? Is this why you've been upset?"

The doorbell rang. "I'll get it," Treha's mother said.

Treha watched as a light dawned on her grandmother's face and the transformation was complete.

"You," she said, turning to Treha. "It was always you."

"I don't understand," Treha said.

"When I talked about you to your mother, when I spoke your name — or wouldn't talk about you. He would get agitated. And he climbed up here and searched and searched."

The woman was crying now, wiping at her tears. Treha put a hand on her shoulder, and her grandmother closed her eyes and shook her head.

"I was the one who made Paige go away," she said. "I sent you away. John said we should keep you and raise you as our own. He talked about you. Wondered where you might be, what you were doing. When we prayed at night, lying side by side, he would speak your name and pray. I asked him to stop. I told him it was too painful."

"How did he know my name?"

"Paige wrote him a letter after you were born. She mentioned that she had asked the adoptive family to keep your first name. He must have carved this pen for you while we were still overseas."

Treha took the pen back and traced the letters with a finger, then looked at the man who carved them. She kissed his forehead. "Thank you for my pen. Thank you for loving me."

His eyes were a faded blue and around the edges were splotches of dark pink and red and veins that were too big. But he smiled again. With great effort he tried to push some word from his own deep cavern, trapped and hidden by layers of boxes and promises and heartache. He struggled to draw it out, his face tightening.

Treha patted his hand and he relaxed. Some words didn't have to be spoken between a grandfather and granddaughter.

CHAPTER 40

Paige

I called Beverly and told her we were coming home. I thanked her for her advice and told her she had been right. Moving toward Treha had been the best decision I had ever made. She said they were planning a reading group get-together where they would welcome our newest member, and I wept when I hung up because it is a wonderful thing to have a friend who knows you.

My father spoke only a handful of words while Treha and I were there, but it was enough to see him content and not agitated, sitting with Treha watching television or just looking out the window. Her presence calmed him and my mother and I marveled at their connection.

We stepped off the plane in Nashville and felt the full onslaught of fall, a new season with new possibilities. As we walked toward the parking lot, Treha put a hand on my arm. When I saw what she was looking at, my heart picked up speed.

Smiling, Ron Gleason held up a poster that said *Welcome home, Paige and Treha.* "Dr. Beckwith told me you were returning this morning. I hope you don't mind."

"I've never had a welcoming committee," Treha said.

"I'm not sure one is a committee," Ron said. "It's good to see you. It sounds like you've been on quite an adventure."

"Thank you for coming," I said, putting a hand on his arm. Coming here was a sweet gesture, kind and thoughtful. The thought crossed my mind then that if Ron was willing to accept and embrace my life, my past, my inabilities, and the ways I'd run from him, perhaps I could run toward him, too. Toward another something good.

"I was thinking of grabbing something for dinner on the way home," I said. "Would you like to join us?"

He smiled. "I'd love it. But let me get the food and meet you there. You go home and get settled."

The night brought laughter and tears. I told Ron everything about the trip, about the past, and it felt like something loosened inside. When Treha yawned and said she was too tired to talk more, Ron put the food away while I showed Treha her room. And then it was just the two of us, finishing the dishes together.

"Are you thinking you'll try to return to school now that you're back?" Ron said as we moved to the living room. "I wasn't sure if I should say anything with Treha here. I didn't want to overstep."

"You'd come to the airport with a sign and you're afraid of overstepping?" I said.

He smiled, taking a seat on the couch in front of the fire. I chose a spot next to him, close to him.

"I'd like to fight for my position there. I think it would be good for me to follow through. With my thesis, the teaching. I really love it, you know? What happened has been a gift. I can see that. The whole thing was something that may liberate both Treha and me."

"What has Treha decided about Bethesda?"

"She's going to leave."

"I see. I can understand that."

"She'll stay with me, at least for now. After the semester we'll both go visit and help my mother with my dad. I don't think it will be long before . . ."

"You want to be a family again."

"Yes. And when I've finished my dissertation, I'm thinking of writing. Continuing to write."

"That's wonderful. What do you want to write about?"

"I think I have something more important on my heart. Treha and me. I want to tell how this struggle we've gone through brought us together. How she brought me to myself. And how I almost missed real life."

"I think that's great, Paige. I'll buy the first copy."

"There's just one thing missing." I waited a bit for dramatic effect. I had practiced this on the drive home from the airport with Treha. She had suggested the silence.

"What's that?" he said.

"Us."

He leaned forward. "Us? I didn't know there was an 'us.' "

"There doesn't have to be if you don't want it."

"Oh, I want an 'us,' " he said. "I've always hoped for an 'us.' An 'us' is more than fine with me."

"I know, and it took the trip and a lot of thinking to realize . . . I wanted to have this conversation with you, invite you here.

When you showed up with that goofy-looking sign today, something melted inside."

He put a hand on my arm and I swear I felt a tingle. Not an explosion or fireworks over Niagara Falls or anything like that, but a tingle.

"I've spent my life rolling this big stone over my heart. Treha helped roll it away. I don't want to live like that anymore. And I don't know where this will lead, I don't know the future, but I know I'll regret it if I don't give 'us' a chance."

Ron smiled. "Wow."

I smiled back. "That's the best you can do? Wow?"

"I've never had an answer to prayer show up on a couch looking so beautiful," he said.

"Kiss her," Treha said behind us, peeking around the corner. I swear she smiled before she ran back to her room.

And he did. He leaned forward and closed his eyes and kissed my lips.

Wow.

There is no greater power on earth than a mother's love, unless it is a child's desire for it. There is no greater power than love that rolls stones away.

After Ron left, I settled into bed and fell

asleep holding a book, dipping again into a familiar story. I was awakened deep in the night by Treha climbing into bed next to me and burying her head beside me under the covers. I turned off the light and hugged her with one arm.

"Did you talk with him?" she said.

"You know we talked. You heard every word."

"Not every word."

"You have to promise you're not going to spy on our every date."

"I promise."

I closed my eyes, night sounds leaking through the window, my hand on my daughter's back, her even breathing lulling me toward rest, toward sleep. And the words rose in my mind. The story of our lives. But instead of waking me, the words soothed and salved the ache, a balm to a weary mind.

When I woke up, the morning sun was streaming through the window, and Treha was still there, sleeping peacefully.

DISCUSSION QUESTIONS

1. Paige believes "there is no greater power on earth than a mother's love," but as the story goes on, she modifies this to include "unless it's a mother's fear" or "a mother's guilt." How do all three emotions — love, fear, and guilt — play roles in the mother-daughter relationships in *Looking into You*?

2. Treha has spent much of her life as an outsider, and while she comes to Bethesda hoping things will be different, it begins to seem she'll be just as misunderstood there. Have you ever tried for a fresh start but been disappointed? What was the result? If you were Miriam — someone who loves and wants the best for Treha — would you have advised her to stick it out at Bethesda or come home?

3. Paige teaches her class that "writing is pain. . . . Writing is joy, as well. Writing is

learning and discovery. If you let it, writing will change you." How do both Paige and Treha process their experiences and change through the written word — especially words they write themselves? Does writing shape the way you see the world or your own life? Or, if not, is it something you'd consider trying?

4. Paige's mother begs her to leave the past alone, arguing that no good can come from revealing herself to Treha. What do you think is behind her desire to keep the family's secret buried? Do you tend to agree with her that the past is better left alone?

5. When Paige learns Treha will be in her class, she considers ways to remove herself or her daughter but eventually acknowledges, "I allowed time and my own indecision to make the decision for me." What do you think she should've done? Was she right to ultimately reveal herself to Treha? Did she go about it in the right way?

6. Treha longed for her mother but found the reality of meeting her different from what she'd expected, what she'd created in her imagination. When have you strug-

gled to reconcile something you've imagined with the reality? In the end, which version was better?

7. Paige and Treha both have people who push them forward — Dr. Waldron, Ron, Beverly, Miriam, Anna, Elsie. Which of these characters did you think were most helpful? Did any of them come on too strong, or too soft, in the challenges they presented? Do you agree with Beverly that "love sometimes looks like a kick in the pants"?

8. Paige confesses to her class, "I've been living under the belief that I have to impress [God], that I have to make every right choice from now on. That I've used up his grace, and one more mistake and I'm through." How do these fears align with or contradict what you believe about God?

9. At a crossroads in the story, Paige wonders if it's fair to force someone else to deal with his or her past. How would you respond if she came to you with this question? What did you think of her decision?

10. When Paige asks how much of the past

she has to dredge up, Beverly replies, "How much of your past do you want God to redeem? . . . How much of your regret and sorrow do you want him to forgive and use? For your good and his glory?" Do you think her "math" here is correct — that God will redeem and use as much of the past as we give him? How have you seen this principle apply in your own life, whether in things you've turned over to God or things you've held back?

ABOUT THE AUTHOR

Chris Fabry is a 1982 graduate of the W. Page Pitt School of Journalism at Marshall University and a native of West Virginia. He is heard on Moody Radio's *Chris Fabry Live, Love Worth Finding,* and *Building Relationships with Dr. Gary Chapman.* He and his wife, Andrea, are the parents of nine children. Chris has published more than seventy books for adults and children, including the recent bestselling novelization *War Room.* His novels *Dogwood, Almost Heaven,* and *Not in the Heart* won Christy Awards, and *Almost Heaven* won the ECPA Christian Book Award for fiction.

You can visit his website at www.chrisfabry.com.

The employees of Thorndike Press hope you have enjoyed this Large Print book. All our Thorndike, Wheeler, and Kennebec Large Print titles are designed for easy reading, and all our books are made to last. Other Thorndike Press Large Print books are available at your library, through selected bookstores, or directly from us.

For information about titles, please call:
(800) 223-1244

or visit our website at:
gale.com/thorndike

To share your comments, please write:
Publisher
Thorndike Press
10 Water St., Suite 310
Waterville, ME 04901